FINAL
LULLABY

SASHA LAUREN

Black Rose Writing | Texas

ISBN: 978-1-68513-257-6
PUBLISHED BY BLACK ROSE WRITING
www.blackrosewriting.com

Printed in the United States of America
Suggested Retail Price (SRP) $20.95

Final Lullaby is printed in Calluna

*As a planet-friendly publisher, Black Rose Writing does its best to eliminate unnecessary waste to reduce paper usage and energy costs, while never compromising the reading experience. As a result, the final word count vs. page count may not meet common expectations.

Dedicated to Dorothy Meghreblian,
my inspiring literature teacher from Junior High School

PRAISE FOR

FINAL

LULLABY

"*Final Lullaby* is a courageous, poetic exploration of a controversial and emotionally-charged topic. At turns uncomfortable and celebratory, artistic and thought provoking, this is an important novel."

–**Brian Kaufman, author of *Sins in Blue***

"*Final Lullaby* is the moving, richly emotional love story of Angela and Tucker, two sweet, artistic souls who embrace life, as they do each other, with unguarded passion. With a great gift for the delicate balance of comedy and tragedy, Sasha Lauren has created two unforgettable, compassionate lovers who dance above tragedy with fearless emotion."

–**David Shawn Klein, author of *The Money***

"Sasha Lauren cuts to the chase in her candid probe of a topic many fictional approaches would shy away from. From issues of medical system corruption that introduce impossible pain to sufferers to the observation that 'heartache is a ravager,' Lauren creates a powerful series of interplays that open with love and move deftly into forbidden territory and subjects that test the hearts of characters and readers alike.

Ideally, *Final Lullaby* will be chosen not just by romance readers who will find the unfolding story departs from predictable paths to enter thought-provoking realms of social inspection, but by book clubs interested in debating many of its issues.

Libraries and readers will find *Final Lullaby* a compelling journey into love, healing, and recovery that operates on different levels, introducing thought-provoking reflections that ultimately demand the reader's engagement on more than just a level of appreciating a romantic interlude and new possibilities of growth."

–*D. Donovan, Sr. Reviewer, Midwest Book Review*

"I would recommend this book to a reader who seeks a novel with depth in characters that will engage your emotions to the end."

"Final Lullaby is a unique love story that evokes powerful emotions and encourages soul searching regarding choices we make when there is no longer quality of life. Amid the beautiful prose and moving poetry, there is a gently laid, intelligent and poignant probe of issues that affect our capacity to accept life when hope is fleeting. Even the deepest of love can't conquer all, but it can provide a guiding light in the darkest hours. Powerful, emotional, heartrending, *Final Lullaby* is a love story I will read again and again."

–Rebecca Warner, Amazon best-selling author of *My Dad, My Dog*

"Sasha Lauren shows her mastery of addressing the difficult topics of the right to die with dignity and medical malpractice through showcasing the pain and suffering of both victims of medical mistakes and the heartbreak of those who love them. No matter a reader's personal opinions on the right to die topic, they will certainly have their eyes opened to the pain and suffering that drive people to a choice no one wants to make."

–Author Barbara A. Luker

"This is an important book for many reasons! It makes you think, listen and feel for what some people deal with and the decisions with which they grapple. Sasha Lauren writes so well she kept me in the story from the beginning."

–Kathryn Jarvis, author of *A Red Door*

Thanks to: Laurie Sutherland of Island Books, Middletown, Rhode Island. Medical malpractice consumer safety advocates and activists in California and the world over. Right to die educators and activists. Former clients and colleagues from my days running Epiphany Scripts. Anyone who is honest, kind, and really listens. Musicians and artists who color life with joy.

Additional thanks to:
Reagan Rothe and the entire team at Black Rose Writing

Kay Dean at Fake Review Watch.
http://fakereviewwatch.com

Mad in America – Science, Psychiatry and Social Justice.
http://madinamerica.com

Lisa McGiffert at Patient Safety Action Network. Thank you for publishing my paper.
http://www.patientsafetyaction.org/wp-content/uploads/2022/11/Lipo-Research-Sasha-Lauren-2022.pdf

Cover Art by Sasha Lauren

FINAL
LULLABY

I.

TUCKER AND ANGELA

Tucker was the most gifted person I ever met. I mean, he seemed normal at first: nerdishly handsome, dressed in a crisp short-sleeved white tee, black jeans, black loafers, and large, black-framed glasses that magnified his long eyelashes. He shook my hand and we introduced ourselves. It was at Rosemary's twenty-ninth birthday party. After ten of us literally scared the crap out of her by yelling "*Surprise!*" from the foyer of her tiny first floor apartment, she had to go to the bathroom. She was gone for seven minutes, and then we all went out for Thai food.

We proceeded to embarrass her by singing a raucous round of "Happy Birthday" in the restaurant. Rosemary then gathered her cards and tchotchke gifts and we ambled back to her quaint, (ahem, claustrophobic), cave to kibitz. Kibitz is a Yiddish word that means to make small talk or idle chatter. I don't know any languages fluently other than English and pig Latin, just a few words here and there, which I like to use whenever I can. I plan to learn Italian someday.

Anyway, back to Tucker. When we all got situated in Rosemary's cramped quarters on wobbly folding chairs, lumpy pillows, or the cat hair-covered floor, Tucker, on the loveseat, reached behind him and grabbed her dusty guitar. As he tuned it, sliding his beautiful, calloused fingers expertly up and down the neck, which believe me was a concert in itself, he smiled and sang Muddy Waters' "Mannish Boy." I thought it was a peculiar choice, but no one else seemed to think so. They all joined in yelling, "yeah, boy," and howling like tigers caught in a trap, just at the right places. I didn't yell or howl though because I felt shy around Tucker.

The crowd clapped and requested songs, but Tucker declined most of them. He said he only wanted to play the blues. "Why only the blues, man?" Koresh asked. "The authenticity makes me happy, man." And with that he played another five bluesy tunes. I knew what he meant about feeling happy because that is how I felt listening to him, hooked on the music and the musician.

As the evening came to a close at nine, Tucker asked me if I wanted to go back to his house to talk. I figured that talk was code for sex, so I said no. Rosemary overheard our conversation and said, "Angie, you should totally go if you want. Tucker's cool, he's safe, I think you'd love his place." That's all it took for me to say yes. Nine was too soon for the evening to end. I was not under the influence of anything but the music and wanted to get to know this exultant blues singer better.

"Okay, sure, but I should leave by ten. What's your address?" He punched his name, number, and address into my phone and handed it back with aplomb. Aplomb is an easy coolness that only a cute blues singer in a crisp white tee and round black glasses can pull off. "Ten thirty," he countered. Rosemary gave a nod of encouragement. I'd known her since sixth grade so I figured she'd know if Tucker and I should hang out, but then on the way to his house I wondered if maybe this was her way of getting back at me for the surprise and singing.

Derby Road, the street Tucker lives on, is lined with spicebush and crabapple, Kousa dogwood, and red maple trees. The aromatic white, red, and yellow floral display is quintessential New England. Reflective stained-glass panels of two winged hearts adorn large square windows on either side of his front door. I knocked with much more moxie than I felt.

"You made it," Tucker took my hand as though helping me out of a luxury limo. I stood face to face with this shining mystery man I'd met ever so briefly at the party of a childhood friend and could only giggle in response to his grin. The two of us would make lousy poker players.

"Come in. This is it." He gestured widely. "Would you like something to drink?" Something to drink may include any sort of beverage. "Would you like a drink?" would mean alcohol.

"Water, please. No ice." The first thing I noticed was that his place was clean, not like my last boyfriend's place. John was a slob. John actually liked to be called Jack, as if he were a Kennedy or something. *Boyfriend!* Was I already thinking about Tucker as my boyfriend? Criminy! I just broke up with Jack two months before. *Don't bite your nails, Angie.* I clutched my hand like I was cracking my knuckles. I imagined introducing Tucker to my parents over a home-prepared shrimp parmesan salad when I spotted a dog dish. Heard a bark. *Pinch me, he's a dog lover too!*

Tucker led me into the kitchen. A black and white marble island stood clumsily in the way of everything, if you ask me (but no one did). Everything else was perfect: black and white tiles, Morris & Co. rose, vanilla, and wine wallpaper and fresh lilies in a vase. Cars swooshed by. He handed me water in a tumbler that reminded me of the frosted lemonade set of my childhood. I downed it like gin. "Another?" he asked.

"Yes, thank you." I held tightly to the glass to keep my hands occupied. A boisterous black lab bounded in and greeted me like we were old friends, which sent the glass tumbling out of my hand. It shattered, pink shards on sparkling tiles.

"Socrates!" Tucker cried. "Down, boy! Down!"

"Oh, no, I'm so sorry." Socrates continued to leap on me, licking my face in welcome.

"No, I'm sorry. Socrates, don't knock over my special guest." Tucker grabbed a broom and swept as Socrates and I danced.

"It's okay," I said. "He just caught me off guard. He's adorable. We're buds now, aren't we, boy?" Socrates barked in agreement.

Tucker showed me his house with the earnestness of a bighearted lap dog who only wants to share himself and be loved. This musician had two guitars, a ukulele, banjo, piano, congas, maracas, and a line of harmonicas. He lingered lovingly over his vintage LP collection, sampling for me one of his favorite songs, a quirky, catchy rendition of Jimmy Cliff's "Sitting Here in Limbo" by Jerry Garcia and David Grisman.

"It's not the blues but listen to how beautiful this is." He closed his eyes and was transported, lost in fingerpicking awesomeness. While his lids were closed, I peeked at his bookcases, which teemed with Vonnegut, Dumas, Steinbeck, and Shakespeare.

Is it possible to fall in the love the day you meet someone? I decided yes.

"I sleep there in the loft. I built it myself."

"You're so talented! It looks comfortable." My tongue stuck to the roof of my mouth as I spoke. Where was that gin when I needed it?

Tucker continued unfettered. "It's very comfy. I'm a photographer. This is my favorite shot. It's a Kestrel in Brooklyn." The photo caught the full spectacular sweep of the hawk's flight. Beneath it sat a photo of a woman's face.

"Who is this? She's lovely." My heart pounded.

"That's Sheba, my wife."

"You're married?"

"I'm a widower."

"Oh. I'm so sorry, Tucker." This was the last thing I expected a young man to say. The pair of them couldn't have been much older than me. Thirty. Thirty-three tops. My mind ran through a panoply of possible scenarios for her early demise: cancer, car accident, suicide.

Tucker tenderly put his arm around me. "Let's go out back." It was a moonless night, but the stars shone bright. The yard was small and well kept. Geranium boxes lined the porch. An Orien telescope leaned against the porch rail. Tucker peered through, adjusted it, then guided me to look. "See that cluster?" I nodded. "That's Canes Venatici. It contains about half a million stars."

"It's beautiful. Wow. You know a lot of things, Tucker."

"I don't know your last name. I don't know what you do or what you love. I don't know what the protocol for grief is."

I looked from Canes Venatici to Tucker. "Alexander. I own a bookshop where I sell coffee and crystals - Bean There, Done That. Bean. B E A N." He laughed. "I thought it was a cute name. What can I say? There's not a massive market for rose quartz or indie bookshops these days, but I do all right. I have a degree in psychology, certificate in gemology, and my favorite thing to do is to listen to people and let them know they're heard. I love streets lined with spicebush, dogs named Socrates, stargazing, sprinting, and singing. There is no protocol for grief. Or life. Or love."

"Wow! Bean There, Done That is legendary. I've been there. We never met though. I'd have remembered you." He moved a piece of hair behind my ear. It wasn't even out of place. "Angela Alexander, I'm Tucker Boyd. This is the most awkward and best first date ever."

"Oh, is this a date?"

"Yes, Angela Alexander, who is very good at playing coy. It's the end of a short date." He consulted his phone. "It's ten thirty. You have to go home now."

But I didn't go home. We went inside, sat on the couch and talked for seven hours until sunrise.

When I was six, we got a sassy Seal Point Siamese kitten, Simon. He strut like the King of the Jungle. His bravado masked his vulnerability. I was mama lion; he was my cub. One afternoon Grandpa Henry made sure all mitts, balls, and bats were cleared from the driveway before he backed out after our Saturday softball game, but he didn't check for the cat. His Land Rover rolled right over Simon. Since then, I've felt an urgency, a sense that time moves at warp speed, and I have to do something significant before something flattens me. It's one reason I run an hour a day; I like to speed up my heart until it pounds in my chest, then slow to a trot until my cheeks pale. That need to speed-run calmed when I met Tucker. *Madeleine would approve of him*, I thought.

The day I met this photographer, blues singer, loft builder, amateur astronomer, young widower, who had visited so many places and seen so much in thirty-two years, I decided to heck with limiting myself to Bean There. I would follow my heart's desire to counsel and console. Listen and love. I already did that at the bookshop by attending to the lovely, lonely, and lost who came in search of crystal cures and Walt Whitman's words and confided to me their dreams and fears.

After I got my master's in psychology at twenty-three, I bought Bean There to provide a living I loved while I gained life experience. I was hesitant to get caught in the health insurance cyclone or cater only to clients with cash to burn. I support everyone, regardless of social standing. Since Jack and I split, I was ready to change things up. I called Carrie Okazaki, who I had met in school. Carrie works at the Take Conscious Control Institute in Montana. She was eager to talk.

"I hate it here," she said." Doctors layer the clients with anti-depressant and other medications, causing problems for people. Many of the therapists and nurses know the diagnoses are detrimental and for insurance purposes, but the code of silence has us muzzled. We fight to support individuals and have rare successes. Don't fall into this trap, kid. Find another way."

Tucker was impassioned about taking pictures of birds in flight. He also staged and photographed homes for real estate agents from New England to New York and food and artifacts for publications. "I have a gig shooting Japanese Arita ware porcelain, dating back to the sixteenth century, for a museum catalogue. Meet me in Manhattan this weekend?"

"That's a long trip. Big commitment. When I go into the city, I stay over *at least* one night."

"Me, too. I drive in monthly for work and to visit my folks in Brooklyn. They have a five-star guest room. Four poster bed, heirloom quilts, and Harry the cat to cozy up with. Plus, a nighttime serenade by Dad and buzzing blueberry smoothies in the morning. What do you say?"

I knew Jack for over a year before I met his parents, and here Tucker invited me not only to meet his, but to break bread with them while I still had sleep in my eyes. "Will they be there?"

"Of course!"

"Won't they think it's weird that you're having me over after just meeting me?"

"Not at all. They're wonderful people. They'll love you."

"Sure!" the word flew out of my mouth as my heart fluttered at the prospect of this adventure.

When I spotted Tucker checking his watch as the train rolled in, my stomach flip-flopped. We hugged, then I peppered him with questions, which is what I do when I'm nervous. "What is your best tip for staging a house? Is it preferable to use neutral tones so buyers can picture themselves living there? Do you make the house smell good? What are your best tricks?"

Sunlight danced off his glasses. "First, declutter and paint. Neutrals bore me. My current project has periwinkle walls, tangerine drapes, and a turquoise Navajo rug."

"It sounds incredible. I'd love to see it." *Really, I just wanted to see him again.*

"I'd be happy to show you. I'd like to see your home and shop too, if you want to show me."

"Oh, of course." The image of Sheba's heart-shaped face in the picture under the Kestrel flashed before me. I have strong self-esteem, but Tucker's talents and the shadow of his wife unnerved me. "Photography and staging? Aren't those two different careers?"

"Staging just happened. Someone asked. I have the skills. I love it. And yes, we baked macaroons."

"We?"

"Sheba baked." I peeked again for an apparition of her. *What sort of sway do those who depart this earth or leave our lives while alive hold over us and affect relationships with those we subsequently meet?* Tucker broke the silence, "Have you ever been to Hallett Nature Sanctuary? It overlooks the pond in the Southeast Corner of the park?"

"I've never even heard of it and I've been coming here all my life."

"It used to be called The Promontory. Do you like birds and beautiful views?"

"No, I hate nature, Tucker!" He appreciated my irony right away, grabbed my hand and pulled me into a run.

"You're in for a treat!" It's a good thing I'm in shape because we jogged for a mile. We stepped into a mystery world adorned with rustic wood railings and useful benches. The calls of egrets and herons and ducks overtook growling motorcycles and car horns. I forgot we were in New York. We could have been on the moon or in a parking lot. All I saw was him.

On our way out of the park, we stopped to see the Cottage Marionette Theatre. "Built in Sweden. Transferred to NYC in 1877," Tucker read. Behind the cottage we dawdled over Shakespeare's Garden of tulips, crocuses, daffodils, anemones, hellebores, roses, and fritillaries, which are darling polka-dotted lilies. Each is a plant mentioned in the bard's plays.

"I have never seen this! How is it possible that this world was right at my feet and I missed it?"

"There are so many treasures to discover in this world. We don't have any time to waste. Have you ever been to the Whisper Bench?" he whispered.

"No. Is it nearby?"

We turned a corner. "Right here."

I bent down to read the placard: "The bench has a twenty-foot granite curve and carries sound from one end to the other." Behind me a woman gave commands to her pit bull. "Sit. Sit. Sit. Sit. Keaton, *sit*." The dog just stood and stared at her with his head cocked.

"Suddenly I feel like sitting," I said. Tucker and the woman laughed. "Are there treats involved?"

"Yes, do you like kibble?"

"Crazy for it. Don't know what *Keaton's* problem is."

They laughed again. The woman continued with her training, "Sit. Sit. Sit. Sit."

"Good luck with that," Tucker said. Then, "Give her a break and sit, Keaton." And he did! The woman, amazed, gave Keaton some kibble and Tucker and I big hugs. Then off they trotted.

"Sit," he said to me.

"Okay, you only have to tell me once. Sit," I pointed to a spot at the other end of the bench. Tucker gave a little joyful sound and sat. So, there I was, having the time of my life without the awareness that I would use the Whisper Bench as a test for Tucker. After a few rounds of *Hi Angela. Hi Tucker. I can hear you. It's a gorgeous day,* I spilled my secret: "I trusted the wrong man. We were together for three years. I never saw the betrayal coming."

Then I walked away and just pretended I never said it. We strolled, enjoyed the foliage, twin jugglers, sunbathers, and feathered sky. After a few minutes that stretched like forever, Tucker held my hand. "Angela, everyone trusts someone they shouldn't at some point in their lives."

"Who have you trusted that you shouldn't have, Tucker?" He counted off on his fingers, politicians, the media, a tax accountant, several barbers, teachers, and a dog walker. A branch snapped beneath me, which startled a baby squirrel who darted between us. We laughed till we had to sit down to breathe. Tucker pulled me up, "Come on, time to meet the folks."

On the train to Brooklyn, panicked at the speed by which the relationship with Tucker was progressing, I closed my eyes momentarily and absorbed myself in a memory of the tiny bookstore Madeleine and I created as kids. In my mind we shelved the doll-sized books and served tea to our teeny tiny customers.

"This is our stop." Tucker tapped me back to the present.

Michael and Brynn Boyd's home is a mash-up of warm and conventional Norman Rockwell comforts and the non-convention of a Bohemian Alley. Tucker's father Michael, a pianist and composer with a 3,000-song repertoire committed to memory, is renowned for his brilliant, lively technique for performing the sonata in D major by Mozart. His mother Brynn was a cabaret singer who toured Europe for a decade before she endured a minor throat surgery for a polyp, which ultimately ended her brief, blazing career. Tucker said if not for that polyp, he and his two-years older sister, Emma, a mambo, rumba, salsa teacher in Spain, would not have existed.

On the train, after Tucker told me about his mother, he told me a Taoist story that reflects the changes in our lives, and the human tendency to assign meaning to each event.

"The story is of a farmer who worked his crops with great sweat and dedication for decades," he began, like a children's librarian. "One day, his prize work horse escaped. The empathetic villagers exclaimed, 'We're sorry you have such bad luck!' The farmer responded, 'Perhaps.' Days later, the horse returned with three healthy wild horses, who were in high spirits. 'This is a miracle!' the villagers cried. The steady old man again responded, 'Perhaps.' The man's twenty-year old son took to taming the stallions, but was thrown off of one, which shattered his leg. The next week, military officers came to the village and drafted every sturdy young male into the army. They rejected the farmer's son due to his injuries. The villagers, overjoyed by this auspicious turn of events, congratulated the farmer on the good outcome. 'Perhaps,' he said. "Oh, look! Here we are! The foyer of the Boyd abode. This is my mother, Brynn. This is Angela." Brynn, who is taller than I expected, taller in fact than Tucker or his father, smelled of lavender. She puffed lightly across the room like a cumulous cloud.

"Welcome!" Brynn kissed both my cheeks.

A four-foot stone plaque inscribed *Mo Anam Cara* faced me head on. Brynn Boyd encircled me with a kindly arm. "There is an ancient Celtic belief that when two souls share a unique connection, they are stronger together than they are apart. When two individuals form a deep and lasting bond, their souls mingle. Each one is said to have found their *anam cara*, soul friend."

Madeleine was my *anam cara*. I never expected to have another one. I shyly avoided looking at Tucker but felt his gaze towards me deep down in my stomach. My cheeks burned as the question of whether Angela and Tucker might be soul friends echoed through everyone's mind.

The focal point of the house is a black grand piano topped with brass and silver framed photos of the family, including a gap-toothed six-year-old Tucker, which tore at my heart, and an older sister. In the living room there are souvenirs from a lifetime of touring and travel, including a copy of their wedding vows captured in custom calligraphy from China, woven baskets from Ghana and a colorful Maasai beaded bib collar. Gossamer Croatian lace overlaid the kitchen table.

Michael is as grounded as Brynn is ethereal. I imagined roots from his feet projecting down through sedimentary rock and granite all the way to the nickel and iron layers and wrapping around the earth's core. He emits gentle strength. His fingers are those of an artist's. Michael served tea in Delftware from the Netherlands - the blue-and-white porcelain earthenware famous since the 1600s. He sweetened mine with delectable thyme honey from Greece.

The hours melted away in three-two time as Tucker's folks regaled me with stories of their creative lives. I learned about Béla Fleck, an American banjo virtuoso who Michael met through fellow musicians in Uganda as Béla was studying the African origins of the banjo. He segued from this story into a history of jazz, which can be traced back to African American roots in 1835 when slaves would gather in Conga Square, New Orleans, to play music and dance on Sundays. In a city with an eclectic mix of immigrants from Haiti, Spain, Africa, France, Britain, and more, jazz continued to develop and flourish. He accompanied every story by a song on the piano, photos, and the welcoming hep-hep-hep laughter of Brynn, my new standard bearer.

This introduction to Tucker's background elucidated for me his breadth of musical knowledge and capacity for curiosity and love. I anticipated him meeting with my book struck parents who quote and perform everything from Shakespeare's Lear to Brecht's Saint Joan with theatricality and joy, which would provide an opportunity for him to imbibe the bedrock of *my* life.

If in fact, Tucker and I turned out *not* to be *anam cara*, I wondered if I could keep his parents just the same? We stayed well into the second afternoon in the kitschy kitchen until his mother shooed us out so we could spend more time alone together. She is one wise woman.

Tucker swung me by the art studio he rented as needed for his photography projects. Japanese folding screens divided the artists' units in the spacious warehouse. Flying saucer lamps clamped onto ceiling beams twelve foot high lit up the place. Two fashion shoots were in progress. After all of the Boyds' culture and charisma, I was appreciably hungry, craving carbohydrates, not my usual fare. "Where can we get the best Italian food in Manhattan?" I begged. "I'm ravenous!"

"Say no more," Tucker pulled me along like a kite. I gleefully flapped in the breeze behind.

"What are your flaws?" I asked him over spaghetti.

He looked stumped, so I offered a prompt. "Are you ever late?"

"No, I value people's time."

"Are you lazy?"

"Me? Pffft. Not a lazy bone in my body. I'm always on the go."

"Are you judgmental? Come on, give me *something*. You can't be this perfect." He swirled his noodles in contemplation, then leaned forward, and rattled off his list, "I cry too easily at movies. I eat in bed. I'm addicted to crossword puzzles. I mean, I can't leave the house without doing one. I can't see a foot in front of me without glasses. I break out in hives when I'm nervous. I take on more projects than I can handle. I interrupt people. I stay up until 2:00 when I plan to go to bed by 10:00. I don't understand football. My little finger doesn't bend, look." He showed me.

"What happened?"

"I broke it playing football."

"Well, none of those things are major flaws," I pronounced. "Not like mine anyway."

"What do you consider your flaws?"

I sighed so loudly that the woman next to us dropped her breadstick. When she got back to her rigatoni, I exhaled *my* list. "I run late, frequently. I'm nearly thirty and haven't done anything with my degree. I sing wildly off key in the shower. I sell crystals to people who believe a stone will change their lives. I got played by my boyfriend and was completely clueless. I'm an idealist *and* a cynic. Today was the best day of my life, but I want to go home and I wish I didn't."

He leaned back with his palm on his chin. The little pinky that wouldn't bend stuck out like a question mark, trying to figure me out. "I'm crazy about you," he said.

Two waiters brought the lady next to us a piece of Tiramisu with a birthday candle in it and sang "Happy Birthday" to her like opera singers. I don't know why, but Tucker and I joined in with gusto. After she made her wish, I asked him, "Would you walk me to the train now?"

I was grateful for the cool night air. We strolled in silence. When we got to the station, I noticed a hive on Tucker's cheek. I awkwardly shook his hand. "Thank you for a lovely time."

Once onboard, I checked my voicemail. My phone vibrated repeatedly when Tucker and I were at his studio, but I don't answer my phone when I spend time with someone. Boundaries, I believe, are a dying art. If I lived with my nose pressed into a screen, I'd miss the real view before me. Four messages were from Rosemary, two from Jack, and one from my best bookseller Daliyah, who began writing international historical sagas at age sixty. So far, she covered India, China, and Siberia. I deleted Jack's messages without listening. *Boundaries.* That turncoat.

"I hope your date is going well. That lost crate of books arrived today," Daliyah crowed.

"Oh, what a relief! Yes, I had a wonderful time. See you tomorrow."

Rosemary and I had spoken briefly the night after her party. In her message, she said she was going out of her mind with curiosity about how my time with Tucker went. He told me that he had met Rosemary on a blind date a year before he married Sheba. He and Rosemary friend zoned each other at the zoo.

Rosemary answered on the first ring. She confirmed. "While we watched the Bonobos and discussed their prolific sex life, I looked at him and said, *friend zone?* He agreed, *definitely.*"

"What, you don't think he's attractive?"

"Of course! I'd friend zone James Bond though."

"Which one?"

"All of them. Attraction is mysterious. You know that."

"Oh yeah, like I was attracted to a lying, scheming player."

"Don't be so hard on yourself."

"I'm upset. Three years of my life down the drain." Some people, and my dear Rosemary is one, think love means shielding people from pain instead of listening, and allowing natural feelings to be. "Angie, everything happens for a reason," she moralized.

"Okay, Rosemary, you know what?"

"No, listen to me. People come into your life for a reason, or a season, or a lifetime."

"True as that one may be, you know I don't do platitudes." A woman across the aisle in a jaunty hat looked over and smiled. *She understood what I was talking about.*

I knew the lines in Rosemary's handbook by rote. I mouthed to the hat lady, *it's a lesson* just as Rosie chimed in, "It's a lesson. Jack came into your life to teach you something." Hat Lady did her darndest to mute her laughter. I motioned for her to come sit next to me. She did.

Rosemary continued, "Good things come to those who wait. There is more than one fish in the sea. When a door closes, a window opens." Then, "When are you going to see Tucker again?"

"I don't know."

"What, you're not attracted to him?"

"I am. Too much. We could have bonobo sex and so much more."

"What's the problem then?"

"There were four of us at dinner. Tucker, me, Jack, and Sheba."

Rosemary sighed, "Breaking up with Jack was a gift. Now you can move on and find your gibbon."

"My what?"

"Your gibbon. Gibbons are apes that mate for life."

"I'm confused now. Am I supposed to be a bonobo or a gibbon?"

"Both. Look, Angie, Sheba's death was tragic. These autumn tides are so unpredictable. She was in the prime of her life and she and Tucker were a magnanimous, loving couple. But now he has a chance to move on with his life. I noticed how he watched you through my entire party."

"He said he blames himself for not going to the beach to surf with her that day because of a photoshoot, but how could he have known? It's been a year and a half. I was his first date." *And I left him pretty abruptly in Manhattan.* After Rosemary and I hung up, I wept briefly onto the hat lady's shoulder. She didn't offer platitudes. She let me burble out my story as she stroked my hair.

2.

GENEVIÈVE AND MADELEINE

Dozens of eager people lined the street, waiting for the shop to open. It was my busiest weekday since December. The mission statement of Bean There is that it serve as an artistic gathering place. We offer book clubs, writing, art, and dance classes, storytelling, and live music. Many groups utilize our event room. Although I participate whenever possible in this constant stream of creativity, I can come and go as I please. We had thirty patrons signed up for the literary book club to discuss *Juggling Ghosts and Chasing Light*, by the distinguished jokester Jonah Dunn.

The shop offers two of the best coffees in the world. Our biggest seller, Antigua Volcanic, is from mountainous regions high above sea level in Guatemala where the sun and ocean winds give the beans a distinctive acidic tone. Supremo from Colombia is popular for its rich flavor and velvety aroma. Locals and regulars drink from the Bean There, Done That mugs I designed. Cardamom, cinnamon, fennel, and clove chai tea is available along with a palate of fresh herb teas and healthy pie slices in environmentally friendly containers.

The "Bean There, Done That, Got the Tee-Shirt" tees are what draws tourists and visitors from up and down the east coast. Wearing them exploded in popularity on social media. On the front is a pretty picture of the entrance, swathed in potted posies and little round tables and chairs. On the lower right is a piece of cloth that reads: "I (consumers' name), have been a patron here since (date here)." We have permanent ink pens so customers can personalize their purchase.

Tourists, locals, historians, and children flock to Bean There, Done That. Celebrity authors make Bean There a destination of choice for readings and signings, eager to meet fans and sell their wares. We showcase fine art by area artists featuring everything from lighthouses and seashells to Chagall-style abstracts, and of course, my well-tended gemstone collection draws a steady crowd. Yet, my most affecting, distinctive touch on New England bookstore life is the accidental invention of Living Story Night.

Living Story Night, in which customers come and talk about their own life expertise and experience, grew organically one night as we were closing down the shop. Lillian Stein, a survivor of Hitler's Holocaust, stayed on as Daliyah balanced the cash register, and I worked on back orders and special orders for the upcoming week. Lillian, like many locals, felt like family to me. These folks, often older, use the bookshop as a home-away-from-home base for their day.

We talked that night about an author who was in for a recent book signing for a memoir chronicling her own mother's dramatic survival of the Nazi genocide. Lillian leaned collusively over the counter and confided to me and Daliyah, "Most of my family was murdered in the camps. Those who survived have quite a story. My last wish to have an audience to tell it to."

"Well, I'd love to hear it now," I said, a proposition Daliyah heartily seconded.

"Here? In the store?"

"Sure, why not?

"Well, because I don't have a book. And it's dinnertime."

"But you have a living story," I said.

"So, I do."

I ordered in Chinese food for us three as Lillian regaled and horrified us for hours. She shared details of her family hiding precious gems, being robbed of heirloom paintings, fighting the SSI men, and ultimately being swept up with hordes of other Jews transported to death camps. Lillian, at that time an innocent of five-years-old, was among them. I inquired if she would be interested in giving her talk at the shop the following week. She was delighted to have an outlet to talk about the breadth of experience from the evils she endured and enchantments she enjoyed.

I advertised the event, and to our delight there was standing room only. A man approached at the end of Lillian's talk. He had been a child in a Nazi household. He wished to tell his story. We scheduled him for the succeeding week. Ever since then, living stories of all sorts have been the backbone of what my bookshop stands for: the acquisition of empathy that broadens our loving relationship with others. The talks resemble an adult show-and-tell with photos or laminated letters being passed around the audience, and clothes or costumes are often used to punctuate the atmosphere of the story of origin. Speakers receive questions from the audience.

Fellow booksellers counseled against our Living Story Nights. They said that authors would become resentful that precious time was being taken away from their book signing slots, which are geared towards selling their books. A colleague in Delaware warned that this would signal the end of my successful era and predicted a sort of art Armageddon. Quite the contrary was true. Living stories became mythical from Maine to Florida and then word spread west. Books of all types, as well as the Bean There merchandise, flew off the shelves as individuals, couples, and families made my store their holiday destination. Some inquired in advance if they might share their own story. My team had the arduous task of choosing who would get the sacred slots.

Early on, one of my favorites was the police officer, former tattooed trapeze artist and prostitute, closeted no longer. *Who knew tattoos could move like that?* Her story was full of heroics and a transformational arc worthy of the finest Hollywood film production. In fact, she is in talks with a major studio about working as advisor with a screenwriter on *An Officer and the Inked Lady*.

During the lunch rush, I heard a female voice tease, "I'd like your most lustrous purple amethyst, please. I understand it will alleviate my sadness and grief and open me up spiritually." I turned to see Geneviève – hat lady - in a purple bowler, pointing to a quality Brazilian amethyst cathedral that looked like an open shark's mouth.

"Isn't she a beauty? It's $550.00. $500.00 for you."

"I'll admire her from here for the time being. Don't be so quick to give away discounts to people you just met on the train, Angela."

I countered, "Don't be so quick to let strangers cry on your shoulder. Daliyah, this is my mysterious travel companion, Geneviève. Geneviève, Daliyah."

"Oh, hey! Angela's told me about you this morning. I look forward to chatting when it slows down." She turned to the next customer, a regular from the Berkshires. "Ooh, Pam, you've got two of my favorites, *Dear Ghost* and *The Man Who Never Died: The Life, Times, and Legacy of Joe Hill, American Labor Icon*. Let me know what you think of the Joe Hill book."

"You need another set of hands. What can I do to help?" Geneviève is a giver.

"Put the books in bags after I ring them up." With that, she stepped round the counter and dove in to work.

Thank you! Come back soon!

Thank you! Have a nice day.

Thank you! The sign-up for the literary club is over there on the wall.

Thank you! Hematite and turquoise. Beautiful combination.

A bookstore at its best is a bastion that brightens souls. The rush of curious minds kept me so busy I barely had time to think of

Tucker. *Okay, so that's a lie.* I thought about him with every breath. Each time the door opened, I ached to see his face.

"Ah, finally, the herds thins out. Let's sit outside and talk, Geneviève. Tea or coffee?"

"Chai tea for me."

Geneviève moves like a dancer. Her hands swirl in generous outward circles as she speaks, like an opening from her heart up to the heavens. I wanted to know everything about her, and she was eager to share about her life, the world, curiosities about me, or just soak in the liquid gold sun.

"One July, my ex-husband James and I stopped in a seaside town for gas."

"How long ago?"

"Ten years now."

"Okay, just wanted a time context."

"Shall I go on?"

"Please."

Geneviève continued. "When we got gas, I asked to walk the shore, which I did, jeans cuffed twice, sand jumping up my calves like spiders climbing chimney pipes, and salt air up my nose. It was such a gift in the middle of a hot summer. James was eager to push through to Portland before sunset for his parents' anniversary party. I wasn't eager at all. The coast beckoned like a delphinium muse.

On the beach, a gull, *like a bomber,* swooped between me and a man walking his dog. The bird ascended with a clam locked helplessly in its grasp. We both gasped, the man with the blue merle toy Shepherds and I. I can't recall if I spoke to him or he spoke to me first as spray misted over us, a blissful ocean kiss. James was napping in our Subaru. He'd pushed the seat all the way back, locked his fingers across his belly, and snore like an old fisherman after a catch."

I sipped my rosehips tea as I listened to her marvelous narration. I now knew enough to stay silent so as not to interrupt her flow.

"'Haaa. That was close!' I said to the man.

'Yes, they do that. Come 'ere, boy,' he called his dogs back.

'He's beautiful! What's his name?' I asked.

He said, 'Homer.'

'As in Simpson, or *The Iliad* and *The Odyssey*?'

'I might not admit if it was the former,' he said, 'This here is Scout. Scout, say hello to....'

'Ruufff.' The dog held out a paw.

'Geneviève. Pleased to meet you.' We shook. Fast friends.

'...To Geneviève.'

"I gave a little clap of excitement. 'Oh, I'm Johnny,'" he said."

Geneviève looked at me pointedly as if to make sure I got the intensity. I did. She continued.

"The cadence was casual, but the impact profound. I glanced towards the black box that cubicled my sleeping sweetie and sighed, glad that we had stopped. We walked, feet wet, then sat, talked about this and that: literature, love, music, the shades of sea and sky."

Then, Geneviève punched the story up another level. She stopped saying *I said, he said* and instead played out both parts.

"'How often do you come up here?' he asked me.

'Four times a year like clockwork. How about you?'

'I walk this beach every day at noon.'

'You never miss a day?'

'No.'

'You're exact? You never come early at 11:00 or late at 1:00 or 2:00?'

'No. I'm always here at noon. I'll see you again when the weather turns.'

"That was my clue our session was adjourned. Throughout the whole anniversary fete of James' parents, the hors d'oeuvres, wine, cake, and backgammon games with our nephews, I already yearned for the months to pass; the slow grate of the wait burned."

"Oh my god," I exclaimed. "What happened? Did you see him in three months?"

"I'll tell you more about Johnny next time. I want to talk about us a bit and then I have to go walk my dog before dark."

"What a cliffhanger, Geneviève! What do you mean by *us?*"

"Well, me, and maybe you. I watched you for an hour today before you knew I was here and thought of our conversation on the ride from Manhattan. You're really quite extraordinary."

"Thank you."

"You mentioned several times that this store is your dream."

"Yes." This is true. It was my dream, but new and unforeseen dreams were on the horizon.

"How does it feel to live your dream?"

"I'm incredibly lucky. I take risks and pour my heart into the store and community. It's fantastic, but I hope to challenge myself in new ways. I'm not exactly sure how."

Jules and Yala hugged me on their way out of the store. "See you at the belly dance class?" Yala asked. I nodded yes.

"Everything you do and what you talked about on the train lines up with my project. I'd like to see if it resonates with you." Geneviève set a notebook on one of the four outdoor white metal tables I'd chosen to set a homelike tone in the shop. The tables have circle cut-outs, which allow streaks of sunshine to beam through. I enjoyed watching the round lights dance on the sidewalk as she turned the title towards me, *North Yarmouth Grief Call Line and Community Support Center.* "It's a non-profit that's been gestating for four years. It's ready to get off the ground."

"It sounds ambitious. What's your premise and how do I fit in?"

"I plan to offer community support in the form of a safe place for anyone needing guidance and assistance. Mental health care has come to mean drugs and psychiatric intervention, which often do more harm than good. Magical thinking and platitudes have also taken hold of society. My vision begins with a call line rooted in love, dignity, and respect with a focus on listening, which is why I thought of you." She awaited my response.

"I'm interested so far, with caution."

"What's your concern?" The shade from her hat rested on the bridge of my nose.

"I used to volunteer at a suicide line. We were told to turn certain people in. This violated their civil rights for consent. That struck me as dirty. People called us with the promise of anonymity, and we were required to break that trust. That system created long-term harm for many people."

"Ah, I understand. I had a friend who was placed on an involuntary hold and pumped with drugs she didn't need, which negatively affected her for years. They harmed, not healed. Would you like to hear me out? See if you're interested if we move away from the old system a bit?"

"Sure, I'm open," I said. "Talk to me."

"All right. The North Yarmouth Homeless Shelter provides temporary beds, showers, food, and referrals, but they lack the ability to provide ongoing support. In time I plan to offer nutrition and cooking classes, dental hygiene, clothing assistance, talk therapy, groups, training in goal planning and decision making, and art, music, and dance classes such as you have here to anyone interested. I'd like to get the community to volunteer to share their skills with one another. The community center will be a place for everyone. No agenda to fix or dispense toxic positivity."

Geneviève might not have realized how neatly this complemented my interests. I decided to hold back my enthusiasm and sound cool and collected. "Do you want to utilize my store for classes?"

"I want to utilize *you.* Here's my card. I'll be at the space tomorrow; eight a.m. Meet me there?"

"Yes. I'll be there."

During our train journey, Geneviève and I both had covered a lot of ground about our lives. She was transfixed by the story of my best friend, Madeleine.

While all the other little girls in my neighborhood played with their collection of American Girl or Barbie dolls, skated like mini derby girls on rollers with big neon orange or lime green wheels, or ambitiously competed against each other in the town's Little Ms. Softball League by aiming the ball *at* instead of *over* each other's heads, Madeleine and I spent our time gleefully obsessed with the golden sheesham and light brown teak wood dollhouse Grandpa Henry built.

Living just two doors down, and destined to be best friends forever, I vowed in a pinky spit and swear ceremony to share my dollhouse with Madeleine since she didn't have a grandpa to craft her one, too. When we were four, our two sets of parents chipped in and outfitted the complete abode with the finest crafted miniature furniture to be found on the Cape, befitting for such a grand, pink roofed palace. At five-foot wide, three-foot long, and five-foot tall, this house became the receptacle for all of Madeleine's and my combined dreams and imagination.

Our dolls slept in double beds with silky rose satin sheets and miniature Native star quilts. Their bathtubs were tiled with colorful Gaudí-inspired Spanish tiles. The kitchen boasted a six-range stove outfitted with a miniature set of carbon steel cookery and a flowered backsplash that matched the petite plants in the garden. The swing and slide set was made with sturdy classic stainless-steel so our dollies could slide with ease and land face first in a puddle instead of grinding to a near halt on a plastic contraption that took all the fun out of the precarious sport.

We delighted in this house for years, only taking breaks to skate, climb trees, and wop baseballs into the sky or outfield, but never quite in the direction we were aiming. During our early elementary school years, Madeleine and I became voracious readers. This is when the dollhouse underwent a gradual transformation into a miniature brick-and-mortar bookshop.

The first thing we did was to fill the bookcases with mini versions of *Treasure Island, Robinson Crusoe, Of Mice and Men, Gulliver's Travels,* and *Little Woman,* books that were sold in sets. After a year, we'd bought all the pre-made sets available, and began to fashion our own. We tried cardboard and popsicle sticks, but neither worked well so we bought doubles of the sets we already had and painted on our own titles. Some were books we'd read such as *The Little Prince, Stuart Little*, and *Harry Potter*, though we passed many a joyful day coming up with our own.

At age eleven, we two became three when a new classmate transferred to our school. Rosemary Katherine Perry was a gangly girl with a messy ginger ponytail and white eyelashes that shaded blue-grey shining eyes. Her chin and lower lip jutted out and trembled just before she burst out in unbridled tinkling laughter, which rang out several times an hour at least. When Rosie, as we nicknamed her, first saw the ever-budding bookstore, one would think that she was at the pearly gates. "Ah. Oh! This is the most *beautiful* shop I have ever seen!"

Madeleine, a cheerleader for everyone on and off the football field, was a pixie girl, delicate and slight like a fawn, with saucer eyes and fine hair cropped to inch long strands that she sometimes spiked up with gel. Those big, loving eyes of her sparkled at me. We glowed with pride over the hard work of our childhood. "I'm going to own a bookstore like this. It will be just like the one my folks take me to four times a year in Rhode Island. Only better!" I gloated.

"I'm going to help her." Little Madeleine piped in. "I'm going to run the book club and read Roald Dahl, Ursula Le Guin, C.S. Lewis, J.K. Rowling, and *my* books to the children."

"Your books?"

"I'm writing a Bunny Boy series about a family of rabbits."

"They're excellent. Madeleine has bunnies and she's a very talented writer."

"Bunny Boy is my favorite. He's a rascally white New Zealand. He understands everything I say. He loves to run through a tube and sit in the yard waiting for me to come home every day."

"Can I see your rabbits, Madeleine?" Rosemary was eager to meet them.

"Where are you going, girls?" My mother hollered after us.

"TO SEE BUNNY BOY!" Our words tumbled over each other as we trooped out the door.

"Mom, can we take Rosie and Maddie with us to the bookstore in Rhode Island next time?"

"Of course. We're going over Thanksgiving break. I'll talk to their parents about it."

From then on, our quarterly family forays to the bookstore included Madeleine and Rosemary, but Madeleine never got to run the book club. While we were backpacking in Europe the summer before college, Madeleine woke up at 2:00 a.m. in a charming, rural fjord village in Norway drenched in sweat with her teeth chattering - click-click-click-click-click-click-click. Rosemary and I heaped our sleeping bags on her and held her delicate head with its slender neck in our hands as we spoon-fed her warm tea. Looking back, we see that she had begun to complain of fatigue, dizziness, and headaches all the way back at Schönbrunn Palace in Vienna, but in our youth, we felt invincible, and we three wrote it off to the rigors of traveling.

We'd had a positive, adventurous trip until then. My purpose in life is to profoundly listen. I work at it. I'd thought a lot about polar characteristics of keeping silent and talking, and suggested we practice verbal mindfulness on the trip, so I came up with a game for us three while we rode through the European countryside. We took turns speaking. We did it for fun and spiritual exercise. One day, for example, Rosemary was speaker and decision maker. The next day Madeleine, then me, and so on back to Rosemary. I made buttons that read:

I'll talk in the future,
And I have in the past,
But as for today,
I'm on a word fast.

We pinned the two buttons back and forth between us, taking several days off so we could all speak at will. The speaker verbally interacted with people, and the silent ones, like Harpo, were quiet, but none-the-less vital. Folks we met along the way would ask, "Can they talk?" We explained the game and pointed to the buttons. People chuckled, patted us on the back, and said they'd like to try. No one lasted long. It's hard not to have your say.

A creative caveat we added is that the silent friends could sing. After we bounded into the back of a train in East Berlin with a gaggle of gorgeous German guys who were, as it turned out, a professional football team on their way to a match, Madeleine stood strong, feet astride, an adorable Audrey Hepburn clone in jean shorts and an embroidered peasant top from Romania, as she warbled out "Wayfaring Stranger," hair puffing in the wind. I could not have been prouder.

The morning after Madeleine got sick, we took her to a homeopathy clinic. With one glance at our pale, slight, clammy friend, the proprietress entreated us to get her to hospital and back home to the U.S. *immediately.* I phoned Madeleine's parents, who flew on a red-eye flight, damn the cost, and took her for blood tests. They escorted her home the next day. Madeleine was diagnosed with chronic lymphocytic leukemia, a type of cancer of the blood in which an increased number of white blood cells exist in the lymphoid tissue. Her case was aggressive. Chemotherapy and radiation were begun immediately. Madeleine, a minor, didn't have a choice in the matter.

Rosemary and I had planned to go away to university, but we both transferred to the local college so we could remain near our fragile friend. Neither of us would have been able to live with ourselves if we abandoned her. Plato said, *The highest form of knowledge is empathy, for it requires us to suspend our egos and live in another's world.* That's what we did with Madeleine.

Rosemary was interested in real estate, like her father. She became a business major. I minored in business, which bored me to tears, to learn the basics of running the bookstore. I majored in psychology because I planned to be a therapist and provide a balm to the sad and struggling.

We, (Rosie and I), often declined invitations to collage parties in order to light off to Madeleine's house. When my schedule allowed, I accompanied Madeleine for treatments. "I'm tired, Angie," she told me. "I threw up twice in my whole life before. Now liquid flows out like the Trevi Fountain. My stomach hurts, throat burns, and I'm so weak, the only thing I dream of is sleep."

Please hang in there and fight, Madeleine. I need you! What will I do without you? The bookshop was always yours and mine together. There were so many things I wanted to say. Some of them were selfish. I was grateful for the word fast training we did in Europe. *Remain quiet.* I counseled myself. *Think of your friend. What would you want to hear in her position?*

"Do you mind if I lie down with you?" She pulled back her blankets, inviting me in. I curled up and circled her bony ribcage in my arms. "Madeleine, I love you. I'm sorry that you're hurting. I'm here for you and want what's best for you. Your mom says there's a chance for remission..."

"My poor mother is desperate and seriously out of touch with reality. She's pushing for a bone marrow transplant even though the doctor explained to us that the cancer has spread. I don't want to go through more of these medical treatments. I wish she would accept the truth and let me be."

I laid my face in the crook of her neck. "She's your mom. You're her precious girl. She needs to hold on to hope. The highest form of empathy is..."

"I know."

I awoke to Madeleine whispering in my ear. "Angela let's talk about the bookstore. That always lifts my spirits. Remember, with or without me, this was always your store. You'll be a great success.

Now, in all these years of planning, we still haven't settled on a catchy name."

Madeleine's mom came in from planting zinnias in her flower garden, which was her piece of paradise and sanity, with two large light blue ceramic mugs filled with steaming white bean and spinach soup. She wore denim overalls with the shoulder straps unhooked, hanging to her knees, and an artificial cheerfulness like a 1950s sitcom mom. "Hello, Angie. How ya doing, Petunia?" She ruffled the one eighth inch hairs that were left on Madeleine's head. "You feel like eating?"

"Sure. It smells good. I'm not nauseous right now." Madeleine scootched herself up. Lena plumped the pillows with such dedication it seemed as though a puffy pillow were a magical elixir to heal her child. She ceremoniously set the cherry wood TV tray across Madeleine's lap.

"I brought you some too, Angela." She gathered up bottles of medicine, a worn copy of *Cannery Row*, and a journal with a pretty paisley cover from Madeleine's bedside table and relocated them to the dresser in order to set down the mug for me. She brought us fancy polished silver, linen napkins, and goblets of lemon water as though we were dining in a five-star restaurant.

"Thank you, Mrs. Miller. I didn't realize how hungry I am."

"Call me, Lena. You're all grown up now. What's in the box?"

"A present for Madeleine." This perked my waiflike friend up.

"A present? What is it?"

"Let's eat while the soup is hot, then you can open it."

"That's sweet of you, Angela. Wait to open the gift until I come back." Lena reluctantly pulled herself out of the room, hating to leave her daughter for a moment, wanting to spend every minute she could with her, and who could blame her?

"Umm, this is good soup. I so rarely feel like eating these days," Madeleine ate a few spoonfuls.

"This is my favorite soup that your mom makes."

"I like the butternut squash, garbanzo bean soup too. Have you had that one?"

"I have. I've *bean* there." This broke us up into peals of laughter. We loved puns.

"Bean there, done that," Madeleine quipped back. "Hey!"

"Hey, what?"

"That's the name of your bookstore."

"Butternut squash?"

"No, silly. *Bean There, Done That.* You're going to serve coffee, right?"

"I guess. I'd like us to keep the coffee offerings simple so we can focus on the literature. No foamy or complicated drinks. I thought we settled on Madeleine and Angie's Book Bonanza."

"Well, first of all, Book Bonanza is an antiquated name. Secondly, it's *your* store now, Angie."

We ate the rest of our soup extoling the virtues and deficiencies of "Bean There." Madeleine, who had been debate team captain in high school, was *extremely* persuasive. "Don't live in denial like my mother. I need you, my pragmatic friend, to be real with me to the end. Coffee Beans. Beans and Books. "Bean There, Done That," it's cute! It's funny. Don't blend in."

"Blend in! A coffee pun!"

From then on, Bean There, Done That was the name of my future shop. No questions asked.

"Angela, finish my soup. It'll give my mom some joy if she thinks I ate mine." As I swallowed the last bit, feeling awkward that we were misleading Lena regarding her daughter's appetite, Madeleine's mother appeared, hair damp from a shower, in a green gauze boho top and brown skirt. I think she was subconsciously impersonating a tree since nature was her steady comfort.

I handed her the box. "Here you go, Madeleine. They are from me and my mom."

"Aw, bunny wrapping paper! I hate to even tear it." Madeleine treated the package with a gentleness often reserved for newborns and puppies. "What! These are adorable! Look, mom!" She held up a pair of soft crocheted slippers in the likeness of a New Zealand rabbit.

"I crocheted the ears; my mom did the rest. These are one-of-a-kind Alexander art."

"They are precious," Madeleine cried. I thought she'd stop momentarily, but her tears did not cease. Mrs. Miller and I flanked her on either side and rubbed her back, passing her tissues until the box was empty. I helped Mrs. Miller walk Madeleine to the bathroom and back to bed. The slippers fit perfectly. "Come by tomorrow after your last class, Angie. I need to talk to you."

The next day when I arrived, I ran into Rosemary carrying the cage with Bunny Boy and Mollie, Madeleine's beloved rabbits, out the front door. Rosemary's eyes were wet. "Madeleine asked me to adopt them. She can't take care of them anymore. See you back at the apartment."

My parents, Phil and Mariana, had moved to join an ex-pat enclave of aging hippies in Costa Rica, and it was time to for me to claim my independence anyway. Rosemary was eager to leave her family, a discombobulation of dysfunction and addictions, so naturally we moved in together.

Madeleine juggled a mass of mixed emotions that year. She was understandably envious that Rosemary and I were healthy, in college, and sharing what she dubbed *The Goddess Den*. She was grateful that we stayed in town to support her but mortified that we changed our lives for her. *You would do the same thing for us, Madeleine,* we reassured her. By her twentieth birthday, after being ravaged by disease and treatments, her skin was translucent, her lips a barely-there pink, head spare of hair, but her eyes were clear, and her presence resembled that of a sage.

There'd always been an air of wisdom about Madeleine. As her physical energy ebbed, she seemed to rise above those of us mired in earthly concerns. After Rosemary left, Madeleine admonished me. "You guys place me on a pedestal. I'm no guru. I'm just a girl who is sick and has had time alone to contemplate life." Then, "Angela, I need your help with some things."

"Of course, Madeleine. Anything. What do you need?"

"I'd like to see Jared." Jared, a chess whiz who secured a place in the Guinness Book of World Records for most dominos toppled, had been her boyfriend since eleventh grade when they tied each other in the debate club finals. She'd stopped receiving visitors (except us goddesses) months earlier. Jared called me at least twice a week, desperate to see her. He feared the worst.

"Oh, thank goodness! He *really* needs to see you. I passed him playing basketball at the park. I can go get him now."

"Fantastic. I need you to help me up to brush my teeth and put on lip gloss. Raspberry, Jared's favorite," she winked. "Wait in the hall and don't let him stay long. I'm tired. There's more."

"All right." She was solemn. I braced myself for what was to come.

"Angela, you're the best friend I ever could have wanted. Now, I'm seriously ill. I'm not going to be here long. One day – soon - I will die. I know you'll miss me terribly, but you'll be strong."

Well, now was my turn to blow through a box of tissues. I'd have given up my lifelong dream of a bookstore, dropped out of college, and word fasted forever to have more time with Madeleine.

She sat up and slipped into the bunny slippers. She wiggled her feet. They fit perfectly. "No one wants to talk about what is to come. It's all denial, lies, and fixes that end up hurting me. All from love, but very sadly misguided. My family is going to topple like Jared's dominos when I'm gone. You know how gentle my father is. I'm his little girl. He will crumble. He and my mom will blame and second-guess themselves. Do you think... I mean... is there any way..."

"What can I do?"

"Keep an eye on them? Visit them. My folks *love* you. They are still so young. I know they don't see it now, but they can have a meaningful life after I'm gone. They were exceptional parents."

I wished Rosemary was there. Madeleine spoke in past tense *as if she was already gone*. I missed her and she was still right in front of me. "I will *adopt* your parents. Tomorrow I'm coming by at 3:30. Your mom has a 3:00 dentist appointment. Will you be okay alone for half an hour?'

"Of course. I'll be fine. You'll be fine. Always remember that. I love you, Angela. Now quick, toss me the barf basin. I'm going to throw up. Then, let's get my lips looking like I actually have some red blood cells and go get that hot boyfriend of mine."

I sat cross-legged in the hall doing calculus homework while Jared and Madeleine lay in bed cooing and professing their love. I heard her say, "Be strong when I'm gone. Life is a game. Play well."

Jared left looking shattered. Madeleine was washed out. She hugged me with surprising strength for one as depleted as she was. She left me with more of her reflections. "I'm the luckiest girl alive. I'd rather have had quality than quantity. Remember, Angela, life is short. Live it how *you* want. Defy the naysayers. Our bookshop will be the best *ever*. Oh, and one day you'll fall in love. You'll know he's the right guy because you'll think, *Madeleine would approve*."

"I love you, Madeleine. I'll see you tomorrow."

"I love you more. Bean There, Done That." She winked.

This following day at 3:30 on the dot, I let myself into the Miller house. I brought two photo albums filled with pictures of me and Madeleine to reminisce. There were shots of us showing off our book-filled dollhouse, doing cartwheels at the lighthouse, having a picnic in front of the Rhode Island bookstore, splattered with paint, at summer camp campouts, trick-or-treating, blowing out birthday candles, at prom, and competing with the track team. A full but short life.

"Hi Madeleine!" It was hard to stay upbeat when I was emotionally devastated, but I wanted to brighten her day. "Maddie? Hello?" I suspected she was asleep so I tiptoed down the hall past the framed photos of Madeleine that spanned kindergarten through twelfth grade, past a gallery of her parent's wedding shots on Nantucket Island, past Ma Joad, the ever-somnolent Ragdoll cat.

"Meow."

"*Shhh.*"

I poked my head round the door to her room. She wasn't in bed. Maybe she was retching into the toilet. My heart sped up. "Madeleine?" I set down the photo albums on the lounge chair where she would lie to look out the window and ran to the bathroom. She wasn't there. I returned to her room, confused and panicked. "Maddie, where *are* you?" It was then I saw the envelopes spread out like a fan on her desk. A swell of nausea tore through me. *Mom. Dad. Angie. Rosie. Jared.*

Oh my god. "Madeleine! Maddie!" I sprinted through the house, beating my best track meet time. I lost all rationality. I threw open closet doors, knelt down and looked under the beds. She couldn't have just *vanished.* "MADDIE!" She wasn't in the house. I dashed outside and headed for the wooden fort where we used to have tea parties. She wasn't in there. The best way I can describe what happened next is a that a sickening calm overtook me. I knew where she was. I went to the side garage door as though in slow motion. It was closed. An envelope was taped on it that read ANGIE. I ignored it and opened the door. Maddie was inside. I had found Maddie.

The paramedics arrived before Mrs. Miller. They climbed a ladder and extricated her neck from the rope that she had used to hang herself. I moved the bunny slippers that had dropped off her feet out of their way as they laid her limp body on an ambulance cot.

After I called 911, I called Lena. "Come home right now. Something happened to Madeleine." She asked for details. I said, "Please just hurry, the rescue squad is here. I have to let them in."

Lena appeared in the frame of the garage door, looking wild. When she saw her daughter's unconscious body she began to shriek,

"Oh my god, Madeleine, baby! What happened? Is she going to be all right?" She lunged forward to reach her baby.

A female paramedic whose tag read "Marley" said, "Mam, step back. She's not breathing. We need to try to resuscitate her."

"Hold her back!" the other responders barked to me.

I put my arms around Lena Miller and held securely, stabilizing a bobbing buoy in a bellicose sea. Firm, present, steady as she blows, breathe-breathe-breathe; she needed an anchor.

Madeleine was blue and not breathing. The emergency team gave her mouth-to-mouth resuscitation and CPR. The blue color paled, but she remained unresponsive. One of them called it. "Pronounced TOD, 3:15 p.m. Official cause of death, asphyxiation caused by hanging."

Lena had collapsed on the ground and sat with her back against a box of Madeleine's ski clothes in a plastic bin neatly labeled by Maddie herself. I held her as she continued to wail in my arms.

The paramedics split up in teams; two went with Lena, and two with me. My team told me I had a level head and a good way of dealing with people in crisis, something that is rare. They suggested I become an EMT. The female first responder, Marley, stayed and wrote down the classes I would need. "You truly have a gift. You kept your head and were there for her. You have the presence of presence. We need more steadfast people like you."

But I'm dying inside. For Madeleine, her parents, friends, me. I phoned Ty Miller. "Hi. This is Angela. I'm at your house. Please come home immediately. Something happened to Maddie."

The rescue squad identified bloody scrapes and bruises on Madeleine's knees and palms and blood on the sidewalk just outside of the garage. The supposition is that she was so weak that she fell on the pavement on her way to complete her last task in life. She was so committed that she picked herself up and carried on. I have nightmares about the terror she felt in her last minutes.

The fact that Madeleine died a violent death alone infuriates me. If I stop being angry, I might just die of a broken heart. I'm not mad at her. No one with an ounce of compassion could say that Madeleine was selfish for wanting to be out of her body.

3.
THE TALK LINE

Tucker's phone rang six times and went to voicemail. I called back. It went straight to voicemail, no rings. Damn it! I went for a six-mile run to sweat out my apprehensions. Came back and found three messages waiting for me.

Hi. Sorry I missed you. I was in the shower. Singing Johnny Cash.

Hi. I'm so glad you called. I'll be up until midnight.

Hi. Where are you? Call any time. You won't bother me. I turn my phone off when I sleep.

"Hi, Tucker, how are you?"

"Angela, hello! I had an amazing time with you yesterday," he gushed. His voice was like a warm rain, comforting and invigorating.

"I know. Me too. I'm sorry I left in such a rush. Apparently, I'm a mess. I don't know if I'll ever be able to trust again." Our words overlapped each other's –

I know. Me too. I'm clear this will never work.

Yes, it's just bad timing for us.

Okay then, as long as we feel the same way.

Yep, we're on the same page.

Then we were silent. Neither of us hung up. I moved about the kitchen, listening to him breathe.

"What are you doing?" he asked. I thought of a list of spellbinding or seductive things to say, but told the truth, "I was eating a caprese salad and listening to "Track of My Tears" when you called."

"Sobbing in your salad, eh? I love that song. Smokey Robinson or Linda Ronstadt?"

"Smokey. Love Linda too, though. What are you doing?"

"I just got back from the city. I'm hoping to buy a stone that will change my life. Maybe a rose quartz? Know where I might get one?"

"As a matter of fact, I do. Meet me at Bean There in half an hour?"

"Okay, sure, but I should leave by ten."

"Ten-thirty."

"Deal."

The next morning, Geneviève and I both arrived precisely at eight. Her storefront consisted of a large paned window next to a bright red door. Across the top of the glass is painted *North Yarmouth Community Support Center* in Garamond, accented by sunflowers, daisies, and Savannah sparrows. She pulled out a lilac, aqua, and blue boondoggle lanyard keychain.

"I haven't seen one of these since I was a kid," I marveled.

"Sarah, my daughter, made this when she was seven," she clasped it to her heart.

The smell of fresh paint, which glittered on the walls, gave me a little high. Mint green. Eggshell blue. The vibes were soft and calm. The wood floor needed refinishing. Under the window in terra cotta pots was a line of yucca, ponytail palm, and jade. This friendly room hugged me in welcome. A quick tour revealed six rooms, two bathrooms, and a spacious, grassy yard.

In an office off the front room, six laptop computers were spaced five feet apart on a narrow wooden desk. Headphones and an ergonomically correct chair were paired with each. "This is the call center." Geneviève handed me a script on paper. My eyes glanced over the words.

I gave it a whirl, my way. "Hello, North Yarmouth Grief and Support Call Line. This is Angela. Hmm...I thought call lines were run from people on cellphones these days."

"Sometimes they are, but I think it's important, if possible, to have counselors focus one hundred percent on callers instead of running around town, taking calls in the middle of traffic. Go on."

"Hi, may I ask your name?"

"Geneviève."

"What's going on, Geneviève?"

"I feel hopeless, despairing. No one understands me. I don't even know why I called. I don't even know why I bother."

"I'm here to listen, Geneviève. Sometimes it's helpful just to talk to someone who cares."

Geneviève sized me up. "You're a natural, Angela."

"No one wants to be in pain or grief. We've all been there and will be again someday."

"Absolutely. Some callers are in acute crisis and just need a friendly ear, but others are dealing with chronic disability or loneliness that has sapped joy and hope from their lives. Some want an escape. That's not weakness. There is an immense need in culture for people to feel supported by a social fabric more tangible than online media and perhaps less dogmatic than religious or membership organizations. Ultimately, I want to create a community support center."

"I love the idea, Geneviève. I'm still not quite sure where I fit in yet."

"I need a co-chair for the board and part time volunteer for the phoneline. Eventually the position will pay. I'm impressed with you, your background, and practical nature." Wow, she was bold.

"I don't have a lot of spare time right now with the store, but I'm interested in learning more."

"Do you have time for breakfast?"

"Yes. I'll swing by the store and bring the book deliveries in. I'll be back in a flash."

Twenty minutes out of town were hand-painted signs along the street, decorated with parsley and tomatoes, that announced *Picky Eaters* 5 miles, then 3 miles, 2 miles, and finally 1 mile ahead. The name *Picky Eaters* is as hokey as *Bean There, Done That*, which gave me some satisfaction. We parked on a gravel road. "Where's the café?" I wondered.

Geneviève pointed to some small structures with thatched roofs set back off the road beyond eleven gardening beds ten feet by thirty-five. Wooden plaques at the head of each bed read: "fennel, lemon balm, rosemary, wild strawberry, spearmint, parsley, oregano, chives, cilantro, cherry tomatoes, scallions." A grandmother in a floppy sun hat directed her grandson to pick some ripe red toms. The little one scampered back to a table and gifted them to his parents. He popped one into his mouth, wincing as the tart juice hit his tastebuds. "Yummy," he approved.

"You get the idea." Geneviève, pleased to have surprised me, basked in delight.

"Yes!"

We ordered veggie omelets. Lemon balm tea for me. Spearmint for Gen. As soon as the waiter left, we excitedly picked our own tea, herbs, scallions and tomatoes. I popped one into my mouth to enjoy the explosion. Eyes closed; I soaked in the songs of the Savannah sparrows.

We covered ground quickly over tea and toast. I went first.

"I learned the nuts and bolts in school. Piaget's stages of development: rules, moral responsibility, and justice. Kohlberg. sleep patterns of adolescents. Dualistic thinking. Vygotsky's zone of proximal development. Oedipus and Electra. Cross-Cultural counseling. Learned behavior. Socioeconomic status and its relation to ideas, behaviors, and values. Social learning theory, preconscious mind, guilt, superego, id, the ego, the conscious mind, and my favorites, the risky shift phenomenon, non-malfeasance, and overconfidence effect. I ate it up. Thirsty to learn *everything*. After I defended my thesis, I just wanted to grow up. Read. Meet people. Travel. I learned more on my own than in school."

"Yes, I can relate. What is your thesis on?"

"I titled it *Suicide Isn't Selfish*."

"Oh, dear."

"What's wrong?" There, I'd done it. Alienated this wonderful woman with my controversial thesis.

"It's just that I think you're perfect for the community support center. I must figure out how to seduce you over to my project."

The waiter brought us more hot water. "Would you like more tea?"

"Yes, please. I'll be right back." I practically leapt over to the lemon balm bed and snapped off a few fresh stems. "This is brilliant! I can't wait to take Tucker here."

"Tucker? The new fellow? I thought you were too raw from your fiancé?"

"Jack? Well, we weren't engaged anyway. The connection was stronger in my head, I guess. I saw Tucker last night.*" Funny how quickly my take on the breakup has changed.*

"What? Tell me everything." Geneviève already felt like a cherished confidante.

"It was out of this world. We're taking it slow. I'll tell you more after you finish *your* story. I'm *dying* to know what happened on the beach with Johnny. You left me hanging!"

Geneviève leaned forward conspiratorially and dove back into her tale. "*Okay...* True to his word, our timing aligned at noon on a Sunday. Scout found me first and held out his paws. *Hello, boy.* I offered him my hands and we danced while James dozed in the car like a king after seven courses. Then I saw *him*, my non-romantic soul kin. Our meetings of the minds had become my raison d'être and mollified my pleasant, though dull, daily grind.

"I pondered, *if he was a woman instead of a man, how might things have been different?* We could have had a friendship without secrets or clandestine conversations. Risk was part of the equation, though I resisted that admission. Love always finds me, Angela. I don't go seeking. It spreads through my pores like a dozen eggs knocked to the floor and oozes its way into a lovely mess, quite at random, leaving me wanting more."

I sipped the lemon-infused hot water and hung on her every word.

"We were given a gift of five years: seventeen simple and sumptuous seasons singing Crosby, Stills, Nash, and Young harmonies, reciting Shakespearian sonnets, discussing the harvest moon and Midwest fireflies in June. I only missed the summer my son Brad graduated with distinction from Stanford, the fall the four of us visited Prague, and the winter my brother died. I let Johnny know I would be unavailable those times so he wouldn't look for me or worry.

"For his part, he never missed a season; he was always there, waiting, walking, and welcoming me back into the fecund fold. Our meetings were perfect. A blithe, bittersweet bequeathal of bits of time, eight hours a year, and all the time in between to dream."

"He sounds wonderful," I mused, thinking of Tucker.

"He was. In December of the fifth year, when we pulled into our parking spot. James decided to accompany me. I wondered how he and Johnny would get along or if a whiff of the wonderment Johnny and I shared might scare the man I married twenty-five years before. I'd missed my solo time with my gull-watching friend in our nine-dimensional worlds, which knew no end.

"As we made our way through drizzle, I searched for the dogs. No Homer or Scout in sight. No Johnny. Just a stretch of silent sand. A woman in a lavender sarong jogged by. The gulls mewed.

"'What time is it?' I asked James.

"'Twelve ten.'

"This meant nothing to him, but the world to me. A wave broke at my feet. Bubbles appeared and disappeared on the hard, wet sand, but still no Johnny.

"'I should've gotten out of the car with you all these years" James drew me close, kissed me.

"'You were right, it's beautiful, Geneviève. Don't let me sleep through it next time.' I finally heard the words from James I'd longed to hear many years before."

A hard rain fell. We retired to Geneviève car to finish talking there.

"I've had a good life," she determined. "University abroad at Oxford, married my childhood sweetheart, had a healthy boy and girl, juggled family and career, and danced a spicy salsa. But nothing was the same once Johnny was gone. James seemed like less of a husband and more like a habit I'd fallen into and couldn't get out of. The library was dusty, the railing leading up to it rusty, the patrons were losing trust in me as I was less patient of their ongoing, never-ending queries. The tan paint on our house was peeling; James thought it looked fine."

I didn't see a wedding ring on Geneviève's finger, and she appeared to be her own entity. I assumed she was no longer married. "What did you do?" I asked.

"Well, by spring, as the sun brightened the soft days, I divorced James in a haze, took that yoga teacher training I'd thought about for ten years, and moved to Portsmouth, my car filled with a few clothes, great-grandmother's chambray rag quilt, and scrapbooks of my kids' pictures and schoolwork. I bought a house up the road from the beach and opened Namasté, a yoga studio near the main street. For the first year I asked everyone about my friend. *Did you know him? He was handsome, wore a hat, had two dogs?* No one knew. It was as if he never existed, lived a shadow life, or was a figment of my imagination.

I adopted a toy Shepherd, Lilly Belle. My classes were the talk of the small town. I made enough money to live simply and comfortably and nurture a gilded garden of lettuce, squash, and strawberries. My kids visited regularly. Sarah and her fiancé - now husband - Ben, chose my town for their wedding ceremony. But what is no longer there still dwarfs what is. Every quarter at noon I still journey up to our beach and walk the shore alone. It's more beautiful than it would have been had Johnny's presence not been known. The beach glass, the gulls, and the private moments of him captivate each and every season. I wear hats now like he did. I bow and say, *Namasté. Johnny, I'll see you again when the weather turns.*"

Her story broke me. *What is no longer there still dwarfs what is.* This life, bewitching and wry, opens our hearts, fills us up, then pulls a fast one, leaving us wondering why. I cried for the loss of Jack, my glorious grandpop Henry, and Madeleine, my dearest friend who skipped more than walked, and sang more than talked. She died too soon for my soul to bear. I sobbed for my beloved customers Billie, Lea, and Aiko, whom we'd lost over the years. Time plays tricks with grief. It flows over and back like waves. Then I cried for Sheba who I never had the pleasure of meeting. Geneviève sat still with her hand steady on my back and let me howl. Again.

4.

SHEBA, JACK, AND MARY ROSE

When Tucker knocked at my door, my shoulders raised in a V. I was self-conscious because one's home is an intimate window into their soul. He'd soon peer at my shelves as I had at his. My hippie style is simple, not sophisticated, but by no means boring. By his reaction, I'd have thought he was viewing the Taj Mahal. "Where did you get this canopy? The tan mesh is exotic and relaxing. Umm, it smells so good, citrusy, in here." He was *such* a home stager.

"Orange oil."

"It's uplifting. A wonderful touch. The pressed flower prints are gorgeous. Did you make them?"

I shook my head, "My best friend Madeleine did."

Then he noticed the stately bookcases, my pride and joy. "So, how does a bookshop owner arrange her books? By height or alphabet?" I appreciated his directness. No snooping in secret like me.

"By author and genre," I gushed. For whatever reason, this delighted him. Jack never mentioned a word about my books.

"Crystals in nearly every window. I am not surprised. You must have rainbows dancing like fairies through your rooms during daylight."

"Yes, and then some! Come see the garden," I pulled him outside. "Though you'll have to come back in during the day to see the full effect." I flipped on the lights that sparkle through my flower beds like stars. "Tucker, meet Mama Rose Quartz. She's a few hundred pounds if she's an ounce. I sit and meditate on her. I care more about rose quartz and sunflowers than furniture."

"I like a woman that has her priorities straight. Mama is spectacular! I've never seen a crystal this size."

"I have three of them." He hugged me for that. No one ever hugged me for my crystals before. Or *maybe* he was just looking for a reason. This taking it slow business isn't all it's cracked up to be, but the two of us with our fragile histories were trying to do the right thing for the long run.

"It's warm out. How about we sit and talk outside? You can sit on Mama. I'll sit here." He lifted a rocking chair from the porch.

I was dizzy with love dopamine. One minute it was 7:00 p.m. and after what passed for fifteen minutes, it was 10:00. *If I keep hanging out with Tucker, I'll be eighty by next week!* We shyly held hands and paused to gaze into each other's eyes. Couldn't help it. After I told him about Picky Eaters, Genevieve, and the North Yarmouth Community Support Center, we dove in deeper.

"How did you and Sheba meet?" I wanted to know all about the woman he had married.

'Lingyun, a real estate agent I stage for, asked me to show a house for him when his wife was in labor. It was a modest place, sort of a fixer-upper, but Lingyun sent me a sales script to recite.

"'As you can see, Bathsheba...

The cathedral ceiling in the kitchen gives it an expansive aura,

The dual skylights provide the dining room with ephemerality,

The landscaped yard is a haven to relax in after a hard day,

The Master Suite comes complete with a fireplace and spa,

The garage allows plenty of space for hodge podge hobbies, and

The recreation room has a full bar with proximity to the whirlpool.

I believe this particular house meets all of the requirements you've been looking for in a home.'

"Sheba, a headhunter with an eye for details, was impressed. 'Thank you, Mr. Boyd,' she said. This indeed is the nicest place Lingyun has shown me so far. Would you mind if I take a few minutes alone to help me determine if it feels like my home?'

"'Certainly, shall I....' I gestured to the door.

'If you don't mind waiting out on the street, I'll come out and meet you when I'm done.'

'All right -- have fun.'

'I shan't be longer than fourteen minutes.'

'Take eighteen if you need.' I laughed a bit uncomfortably at my own joke.

'Thank you, Mr. Boyd.'

"Sheba floated through the foyer and made a beeline to the second floor; she passed through the Master Suite, into the bathroom, past the bidet, beyond the bowl, and straight to the shower. She dropped her bag, pulled out a beige bath sheet and hung it on the door. She disrobed, watch last.

"12:10 p.m., it read. Leaning in, she adjusted the water temperature, hot, but not scalding. The room filled with steam. She removed bottles of travel shampoo and conditioner from her bag, stepped inside the silver stall and sudsed up her hair. With a last adjustment to the water Sheba broke into up-tempo song, tentatively at first:

Once a jolly swagman camped by a billabong,
Under the shade of a coolibah tree.
And he sang as he watched and waited 'til his billy boiled,
'You'll come a-waltzing, Matilda, with me.'

The acoustics were good!

Oh, give me a home where the buffalo roam,
Where the deer and the antelope play,

Where seldom is heard a discouraging word,
And the skies are not cloudy all day

"Fully warmed up now, as much shower-dancing as singing, skin warm, lungs warm, heart warm, she chanted resoundingly:"

Om Mani Padme Hum
Om Mani Padme Hum
Om Mani Padme Hum
Om Mani Padme Hum
Auuuuuuum, auuuuuuum, auuuuuuum

"She turned the hot to off, finished with a cold rinse, and hip-hopped out like a newborn bunny. The steamed watch face read: 12:19. True to form, each song had been three minutes. She toweled off, combed her shoulder-length corkscrew curls, redressed, exited the room, realized she forgot something, re-entered, took her finger and made a jazzy heart on the steamy mirror.

"I looked up from my Scrabble game. A good buddy and trumpet player from my band, Tyrone, was gallingly close to closing the gap on my lead. 'Ah, 12:24. Right on time,' I crooned as Sheba shot through the door energized like the Mad Hatter. With her tan towel draped elegantly over her arm like a waiter at Tavern on the Green, she pumped my clammy hand. 'I'll take it!' She never moved in though. She moved in with me. I'll tell you more later. It's 1:00 already. But what about you? How did you meet Jack?"

"Jack directs radio ads and TV commercials. He came into Bean There a few times for books on film directing and then asked me to do set dressing for a public library spot. He's charismatic like a politician moonlighting as a magician. He pursued me for a year before I relented. You know the hokey commercials with the cow who sings in French about advantages of cheese?"

"Yes."

"Jack did those."

"Wait a minute, you mean Jack *Vyazmensky*?" He sang, "*Ma chère, essayez ce délicieux fromage.*"

"Yeah. You sound a lot better than the cow."

"I know him!"

"The cow?"

"Jack!" Tucker covered his mouth with laugher, his little crooked pinky hooked in midair.

"Oh, no! How? This is... ah... awkward." This reminded me of the classic dream of walking down the middle of the street with my teeth rotting and falling out.

"We worked together on a few commercial shoots. Yeah, Jack, King of the Jingles!"

"Do you know him well?"

"Yes, well enough. We're part of a Poker league."

"You play poker?" Ugh. This was a hobby I had disliked about Jack.

"Yeah. Sometimes I play to socialize on a set. It's fun."

"Who wins, you or Jack?"

"Mostly Jack. He's an excellent player."

"He's a player, all right. Does he ever talk about me?"

"Not that I recall. He's a trip, always singing his little jingles. Oh, wait, he used to sing "Angie" by The Rolling Stones a lot. Maybe that was about you!"

"Yep. He sang that to me constantly. How long ago?" I shuddered, imagining Jack sharing details about our sex life or talking about having a girlfriend and one on the side.

"I don't remember. Maybe in the spring."

"I don't want to talk about Jack anymore. We had a great three years, but... *whatever.*"

"I understand how a betrayal or loss can mess with your mind. I'm trustworthy though."

"I try not to gossip. I recently acquired a book called *Choftez Chiam* by Yisrael Meir Kagan. It's about the laws of clean speech. I'm a fan of listening and guarding one's tongue."

"I admire that. Hey, I have my guitar in the car. How about I play "Angie" for you now? An instrumental version by Bert Jansch. We'll reclaim the song title."

"You're smooth, Tucker. I like how you worked that in. Yes, I'd love to hear it. Who's Bert Jansch?"

"A Scottish folk musician who also plays the blues. Founding member of Pentangle?" I shook my head, lost. "Oh, my dear Angela, I have so much to teach you."

And with that, the taking it slow phase of our relationship ended.

At 10:15 a.m. the following morning, Geneviève called to ask if I would fill in on the call line a few evenings. A counselor had taken ill. Tucker was already up and on his way to a job.

"Sure, I'll be there, but do you think I'm ready?"

"You have your master's degree in psychology and spent your life learning to listen. Focus on callers like you do customers. Jot down names and notes if you want. Most importantly, be yourself. I'm out of town at my daughter's so I can't cover the shifts. Call me with questions."

"Right. Will do. Is everything okay?"

"Meh. Could be better. I'll fill you in later. Mandrel is on the shift before you. He'll let you in, give you a key, and go over the protocol for the phones again. You'll like him."

"Okay. Talk to you soon."

"Angela."

"Yes?"

"Thanks a million. You'll do great."

Luckily, Daliyah and Martin, another of my star booksellers, (a raw uncook book writer), were both scheduled at the store that day. I let them know I wouldn't be in. That way, Tucker and I could spend more time together later. We had to pry ourselves apart when it was time for me to take my first shift at the call center.

I recognized Mandrel Abara immediately. He used to play in the NBA. At 6'7," he towered over me. Now, this former basketball player, motivational speaker, also volunteered his time at the call line four shifts per week. He's the real deal. After Mandrel left, it was odd being in the center alone. I hadn't expected to get onboard this soon.

"Hello, North Yarmouth Grief and Support Call Line. This is Angela. What's your name?"

"Ah.... Erm..."

Click.

"Hello, good evening, how are you? North Yarmouth Grief and Support Call Line. My name is Angela. Who do I have the pleasure of speaking to?"

"Whoa, a little chirpy for a grief hotline, don't you think? Are you new, Angela?"

"Yes. It's my first night. Too much?"

"Yeah, tone it down a bit, I'm dark, moody, called to talk to someone, not to be hit by a f---ing ray of sunshine."

"Okay. Point taken. What's your name?"

"Jacque."

"What's going on tonight, Jacque?"

"Well, it's just a really f---ing, shitty time. Lost my job in February, house is foreclosing, my cat Petruchio has kidney problems and is puking all over the house, I have the flu, I burnt the stew, and then I called you."

"Oh... you have a cat named Petruchio?"

"Ha ha ha ha ha ha. None of that active listening stuff for you, Angela. Good on you. Yes. I have two cats. Guess the other one's name."

"Kate?"

"Ha ha ha ha ha ha. Yes. I feel better already. When are your shifts, Angela?"

"I'll be here Tuesday and Wednesday nights from 6:00 to midnight."

"Cool. I'll talk to you tomorrow. Good night."

"Good night."

Click.

"Hello, um... Hi! ... ah, good ev... (ahem). H...h...hey there, North Yarmouth Grief Hotline and Support Call Line. This is Angela. What's your name?"

"Len."

"Hi. What's going on tonight, Len?"

"I'd like help writing my suicide note."

"You'd... wha... what! Oh, my goodness! You're not going to kill yourself, are you? Oh... do you need... shall we call emergency...?"

"This your first night, Angela?"

"Yes."

"Calm down. Take a long slow breath in, Angela. You're hyperventilating. Breathe in and count to four. One... count with me, Angela.'

"One... Two...Three... Four..."

"Feel better, Angela?"

"Yes. Yes. I think so."

"Okay, listen, I'll talk to you again once you get broken in a bit."

"Okay."

"Good night."

"Night."

Click.

"Hello, North Yarmouth Grief and Support Line. This is Angela. What's your name?"

"This is Mary Rose O'Shannessy. (Sniff.) I... (Sniff)... I... I ... "

"Oh, Mary Rose, what's going on?"

"I.... (Sniff)... Kieran, he.... he..."

"He what, Mary Rose. What is it? What has happened?'

"My Kieran... he... he used to sing to me..."

"Oh, I see. Did he die?"

"Yes, Angela. January 5th at 5:00 a.m. Pancreatic cancer. We were married fifty-eight years."

"I'm so sorry, Mary Rose. Would you like to talk about it?"

"No."

"Oh. Is there something I can do for you?"

"Yes, Angela."

"What is it? What can I do?"

"Do you sing?"

"Umm... well, I... sometimes, I mean, you know, in the shower and stuff."

"My Kieran, he used to sing me to sleep. Will you... (sniff)... sing to me... a lullaby?"

"Yes. I... sure... I can do that, Mary Rose."

"Thank you, dear. He used to sing "My Wild Irish Rose."Do you know it?"

"I know the tune. I can find the lyrics online. Just give me a second. Yep. Here they are."

"All right. Let me just take out m' dentures and get tucked in. If I fall asleep, you can hang up... (Scuffle, scuffle) Okay. I'm ready now."

If you'll listen, I'll sing you a sweet little song,
Of a flower that's now drooped and dead,
Yet dearer to me, yes, than all of its mates,
Tho' each holds aloft its proud head.
'Twas given to me by a girl that I know,
Since we've met, faith, I've known no repose,
She is dearer by far than the world's brightest star,
And I call her my wild Irish Rose
My wild Irish Rose,
The sweetest flow'r that grows,
You may search ev'rywhere,
But none can compare
With my wild Irish Rose.
My wild Irish Rose,
The dearest flow'r that grows,

And some day for my sake,
She may let me take
The bloom from my wild Irish Rose.
They may sing of their roses which, by other names,
Would smell just as sweetly, they say,
But I know that my Rose would never consent
To have that sweet name taken away.
Her glances are shy when e'er I pass by
The bower, where my true love grows;
And my one wish has been that some day I may win
The heart of my wild Irish Rose.

"Mary Rose... Mary Rose...?"

5.
THE MAYOR OF NEW YORK

Before I met Tucker, I'd been in four relationships with men. One during high school, one at Northwestern, one in grad school, and that three-year sordid affair I *thought* was a relationship with Jack until it ended on a sour note. See, Madeleine would've loved the pun about how the milk soured. She'd have called it an *udderly* ridiculous pun, as a nod to Jack's silly singing cow commercials. We'd have referred back to the joke for a week through ongoing bouts of laugher. This is how it is when a close, beloved friend dies. The friendship carries on one-sided.

But I digress. The four relationships I had all followed a similar pattern of escalation. First the cute meet. Then, a period of flirting, including a little game of cat-and-mouse while we ascertained that we wanted to move forward. Next came a few prudish, buttoned up, and proper dates, and then finally the moment when clothes were torn off, boots were thrown across the room, and we loudly and lustily claimed each other's bodies as our own. Like a dog peeing on its territory, a sense of emotional proprietorship of the other came along with the sexual terrain.

I don't do one-night stands or one-sided obsessions. I don't waste time with men whose taste in music is terrible, or if they are overly possessive, or selfish in bed, or have poor dental hygiene, or think that Shakespeare wasn't Shakespeare. When I met someone promising and shiny that I liked who liked me back equally, I dove in, but at a measured pace. I kept my own place.

This is not how it went with Tucker. After the night he played Jansch's "Angie", we were *all in*. Joined at the hip, but independent. Craving to see each other every moment. In fact, we had to set an alarm to remind us to go to sleep because otherwise we would stay up all night talking, singing, dancing, having sex. Yes, sorry, it really was that good. We were lucky, and we knew it.

If I sat and did endless hours of visualization in attempts to manifest the perfect man like Rosemary did, I would never have met Tucker because I didn't even know that a person like him existed. I don't mean to make it sound like he was flawless, because he wasn't. As brilliant as he was in his Renaissance ways, he couldn't balance his checkbook to save his life. He just took the bank's word for it every month, crossed out *his* number, replaced it with theirs and highlighted the new total in fluorescent green. Green for money. He was jumpy and grumpy in traffic, especially when I was driving. He'd perch on the edge of his seat and scrutinize parallel traffic as though he was searching the sky for a hawk flying by to photograph.

"You're as bad as my mother with your backseat driving," I told him. "Back off, buddy. Quit micromanaging. Do *you* want to drive?"

But for all his little quirks and faux pas, Tucker was a saint and everyone knew it. He looked deeply into everyone's eyes, fully present, gleaming with glee, and allowed you to see the world as he did: a luscious, loving, divine realm in which you were seen, lifted up, and vowed inside to be a better person. He was the holy man on the mountain in the middle of Manhattan.

Although he was protective of getting a solid seven hours of sleep, Tucker was like a small hurricane who never really tired. His mind was turned on to the world; his heart beamed out acceptance and joy. To know Tucker was to love him. I'm intellectually and emotionally open too, but I considered myself more of an introvert, and all the personality tests – Briggs-Meyer, Disc, Enneagram, and Big Five –put me on the cusp, just over the line of contemplative.

I like to run, meditate or garden in my yard, visit with friends, occasionally go to plays and hear live music, and primarily run my store, getting lost in the worlds of literature and gemstones, a dreamer, existing as much in an ethereal dimension than this one. Before Tucker, I lived for cozy nights in around the fireplace, reading, petting the cat, and dozing off to Daniel Barenboim playing Chopin's "Étude Op. 25. No. 1 in A Flat Major." That was all the excitement I desired.

Then Tucker blew in.

The way he grabbed my hand and pulled me to the bird sanctuary in the park on our first date is the way it was from then on. I was glad to gust along, setting my toes in the shadows of Tucker's heels as we explored this fascinating world together. No personality test was needed to tell me Tucker was an extrovert with a capital E. He'd shake hands with a healthy pump, then pull friends and strangers alike into a tight embrace. He petted dogs and flew babies in the air like little starlings in the breeze, played hopscotch and wrestled with kids, and tutored teens. He knew half the people we met and the others wanted to know him.

"What are you, the mayor of New York?" I marveled.

"Hold your tongue, Angela. I would never survive in the political world. The hawks would pick over my ethical carcass. I'm glad we're both Independents. No sides. Power to the people."

"Right on." At our first concert together, I took hold of his hand and towed him along. "Step on it, mayor, the doors are open. Let's wiggle and waggle our way down to the front row." Then we danced, arms up moving to the reggae beat, mon. It was the same way at home. Tucker was a one-man band, moving effortlessly from keyboards to guitar to drums. He had a green two-foot by three-foot chalkboard in his living room with a list of random words scribbled all over it.

"What's this for, mayor?"

"That's my *Jeopardy!* board."

"*Jeopardy!*, the game show? do do do do do do do, do do do do DUT da do do do do..."

"Yes, that's the one. Quick, come here, Cheesecake. It's on in a minute."

"Cheesecake?"

"You gave me a nickname; I gave you one."

"Why Cheesecake?" *I wasn't so sure I liked this name.*

"Because you're sweet, and I can't get enough of you."

"Aww."

"Shhh. Here we go. I bet you're great at this game. You must have a lot of trivia stored up in that book-reading, intellectual noggin of yours."

"Oh, mayor, you got that right. Get ready to be creamed in this game."

Ooo, ooh
What is the Eric Canal?
What is The Cherry Orchard?
Who is Mama Cass Elliot?
Who is Fyodor Mikhailovich Dostoevsky?
What is an armadillo?
What is String Theory?

Tucker and I were both wildly competitive. We played *Jeopardy!* like we were fighting for seats on the lifeboats of the Titanic. Fists pumping in the air when we got the right question. When he didn't know an answer, he turned around, grabbed a piece of chalk and wrote it on the board to look up later, which he did. As fierce as our sexual chemistry was, our mutual thirst for knowledge was as much a turn on as anything I had ever felt in my life before.

What is Imotski, Croatia?

"What! How do you know that?"

"I went to Eastern Europe to go bird watching."

"Where haven't you gone? Are there any places left for us to go together?"

"Oh, so many, Cheesecake. We have the whole world to discover together. I already have some ideas of where we can go. We can make a list on the right side of the board."

I turned around, picked up a piece of pink chalk, and wrote, *Imotski, Croatia.*

"You want to go there?"

"Perhaps. For now, I want to look it up. I don't know anything about it."

"Croatian avifauna consists of 387 bird species, of which 233 species are nesters; 178 species are classed as threatened on the national level, 69 on the European level and 21 on the global level."

"Okay, Mr. Show Off. Shh. It's Final Jeopardy. I slay at Final. I'm going to bet everything."

"Oh, you are, are you? You're going to bet all your fake money?"

"The winner gets to choose the first international destination for our first international holiday together."

"Oh," Tucker said, "and, and, and be sexually *ravaged* by the loser."

The category is Nineteenth Century Novels.

"Oh, no, I'm screwed."

"Literally," I gleamed.

In a book by Alexandre Dumas, **he**, *the swashbuckling hero based on a real person, left his home in Gascony to make his way to Paris.*

"Who was D'Artagnan?" I screamed, pumping my fists as though I was trying to break down an invisible concrete wall.

"OOOOOH. I KNEW that!!!"

"Not as fast as I did, sucker. Get your bags packed for a south-of-the-equator vacation."

"Where are we going?'

"I will tell *you*, mayor, later. You've got some ravaging to do first."

I ran to the congas and played a *pod-a-pete, pod-a-pete, pod-a-pete* beat like Tucker did when he got an answer right, or when the sun rose in the morning, or when the moon appeared at night.

6.
ROBBY AND NEIL

There are some people who possess such concrete wisdom, highly developed empathy and intuition, and are achingly adroit and masterly in at least one craft or calling at such a tender age that the term *old soul* seems not only fitting, but essential in explaining the phenomenon of the exceedingly evolved human being. I'm sure that solid influences and good parenting help, but in the case of Robby Delagua, after five minutes of conversation, my *old soul* antenna was up.

Robby called at 11:50 p.m. on the slowest night I'd had at the hotline. There were only about two calls an hour. The first caller that unusually quiet evening was a shy or discreet person, or perhaps someone so achingly troubled they were incapable of putting words to their sorrows.

"Hello, North Yarmouth Grief and Support Line. This is Angela. What's your name?"

Silence

"Hello... is anybody there?"

"Um."

"Hi, are you in any physical danger?"

"Ummm umm."

"Are you feeling sad?"

"Umm huh."

Silence.

"Would you like to talk about it?"

"Ummm umm."

"Do you feel suicidal?"

"Ummm umm."

"Okay. I'm here. Take as long as you need."

We held on in silence for five minutes, which felt infinitely longer as my senses remained acute and ready to respond in whatever way this caller needed me to. The poignancy throbbed in the quietude. I heard a faint sad exhale, a slight scratch of a chair, and then a profound stillness in which we two were anchored together in our vulnerable, imperfect humanness.

"Thank you," the voice said finally.

"You're welcome. I'm here Tuesdays and Wednesdays from 6:00 p.m. to midnight. Call me anytime."

Click.

In between calls I balanced end-of-month finances for Bean There, went through ten pages of the publisher's catalogue, sent emails about the spring award programs, and organized a discounted delivery for underprivileged families. I started on backorders and specials for the week, but Tucker called several times. I grew fidgety, so I stretched and did sit-ups and push-ups.

"Hi, mayor, how are you?"

"Hi, sweets, I'm great. Rosemary and her new guy Scott came by. We played cribbage, and I won. Had a few laughs too. Rosie told funny stories about her cat."

"What did Penelope do now?"

"Whenever she hears The British National Anthem, the poor thing howls and runs in circles. That Rosemary sure tells an animated story."

"Yeah, she's hysterical. Her cat is a nervous wreck. I wonder what Penny has against Britain?"

"Nothing, the puss just has sophisticated musical tastes. She sidles up and purrs when I play Elmore James. Now I'm organizing bird photos. I'm intrigued by your idea of putting together a photography book accompanied by narratives of when I got the captures. How's it going there?"

"I'm bored. I can see why grief chatlines are set up so people answer from their cell phones. I have to talk to Geneviève about this. The number of calls varies so much. Mandrel says *just wait; the holidays will be hopping.* Oh, hey, the line is ringing now. Gotta go. I love you."

I hung up in the middle of Tucker saying, "I love you too," then completely switched gears from lovestruck girlfriend and segued into calming counselor mode. "Hello, North Yarmouth Grief and Support Line. This is Angela. What's your name?"

"Hi, did you say your name is Angela?"

"Yes."

"I'm Robert. Robby. How long do I have to talk? Are you busy on another line? I have a lot to say. I've never called a hotline or warmline or whatever ya call it. I'm just going to talk, I guess, to you, a woman I never met and pour my heart out because I don't know what else to do. I usually talk to my parents, coach, friends, girlfriend, but no one understands what I'm going through. When I try to explain to them, they minimize my situation. It makes me feel bad that I'm struggling, like I should magically be okay, but people aren't like that, ya know? They try to placate me by saying everything is going to be okay, ya know? That's bullshit because they don't know that. Oh shit, is it okay if I say bullshit? I don't usually swear unless I'm all worked up."

He sounded young, but I sensed he had a piercing view into human behavior, even during his crisis. I didn't often get calls from minors. "No worries, Robby, sometimes things are bullshit. Use whatever words you need to." I thought of the last caller who couldn't even speak.

"How long do I have to talk? I know it's late and all."

It was midnight. My body was aching to crawl in bed with Tucker and Socrates, those rambunctious rascals who hogged all the blankets. "Take your time, Robby. Obviously, something significant is bothering you. I'm here to listen."

"*Hooooo.* Thanks, Angela. Will you just promise me one thing?"

"What?"

"The ad for your call line says that you listen. That's what I need. No advice. No placating. No motivational quotes or warm and fuzzy sayings. My life sucks. Don't talk me out of it."

"I promise. You got the right person here. What's going on?"

Robby spun through his life for me, which had been mostly charmed up until the week before when this Homecoming King, honor student, high school star quarterback with his eye on a professional football career was running the bleachers during football training session, and slipped off the end. The impact from the fall shattered his left leg in several places.

"It happened in a second but seemed like forever. My unlucky leg kind of broke the fall. At first, I didn't feel anything. Shock. Coach Ken hollered, 'Call 911!' He knelt next to me, felt my pulse and said, 'Don't move, buddy. You took a big fall.' Then the pain kicked in. Coach kept his eyes locked on me. 'I'm right here with you, buddy. You're going to be okay. Help is on the way.' My teammates looked like a grove of redwood trees hovering over me. Their pupils were wild and dilated. Sirens screeched in the distance. They were for me. It was like a nightmare. I just wanted to wake up from it. Coach yelled, 'Get back. Let 'em through.' Six big strapping guys in big brown boots and jackets, firefighters, I guess, hooked me up to beeping monitors and shit. It's all a blur. I vaguely remember the smell of the grass, blood on my palms. They lifted me all crumpled up onto a stretcher. I screamed when they moved me. They doped me up with something. I woke up in the hospital. Had my leg operated on the next morning. I'm in a cast up to my ass. Bedridden. Gonna have to relearn to walk. I'm in such bad pain I can hardly sleep. I don't want to take the drugs. My future career is ruined. Football is all I ever wanted to do."

I texted Tucker. *Don't wait up for me. I got a kid on the line whose life was just shattered. I don't know how long I'll be. I can go to my place if you want. Sorry.*

He texted back. *Spread your healing, my love. I don't want you there alone at this hour. I was already on my way to surprise you. Open the door for me.*

My focus was on Robby, so I just wrote *okay.*

"That's terrible, Robby, I'm so sorry. I'm tempted to say something soothing, but it would be patronizing, and I promised you I wouldn't."

"Thank you, Angela, for keeping your word. Whenever I talk about the pain, people want to shut me up, medicate me up, lift me up. I just need a safe place to talk, to bitch and moan and not be judged for it. Because you know what? It is fucked up. There is nothing good about this. The storm loosened part of the guardrail. The steps were wet after the rain. I slipped."

"Was this at North Yarmouth High School."

"Yeah."

"I used to go there. Now I run the bleachers on the weekends sometimes. I saw the damaged rail about three weeks ago. Is that when this happened? What do the doctors say your prognosis is?"

Tucker tapped at the door. I ushered him in with a *shhh* finger to my lips. He winked and handed me a mug of rosehips and lemon tea. The hot liquid warmed my esophagus and stomach. I was so caught up in Robby's story, I hadn't noticed I was shivering. Tucker slipped my pearl grey Aran cable crossover neck sweater over my head. He thought of everything.

As Robby continued talking, Tucker dragged a love seat into the phone room. We curled up on it. "Twenty-four days ago, Angela. I started physical therapy, last week. A gruff woman named Marta beats me up a little. I'm not gonna lie, she seems a bit sadistic. I can't imagine how I will ever get my athletic body back. I think the doctors are bullshitting me. They say *we can't guarantee anything but... ya know... keep at it. You'll progress steadily. Hang in there.* When I question them, they act like I'm an idiot that doesn't know anything about my body. And they don't have any guarantee. Did you ever have anything broken, Angela?"

"Just my heart." Tucker, who was now lying with his head in my lap, reached up and touched his fingers to my cheek, then closed his eyes and fell asleep as though put under by a hypnotist.

"Oh, sorry, that sucks too."

"Well, it's not like a shattered leg."

Robby shared his story with me without shame. I didn't want to interrupt him. We talked until 3:00 a.m. I curled up next to Tucker and we slept knotted together for six hours until the door chimed and in walked a man of about forty-two. He had an obsessively neat beard and mustache, plaid coat, and old-fashioned bowler hat. He looked like a P.I.

"Whoa!" He stepped back a with a start. His coffee sloshed on the floor. "Who are you?"

I leapt up, heart pounding. "Hi, I'm Tucker. I mean, I'm Angela, this is Tuck..."

Tucker, like the "mayor" that he was, stood up cool, calm, and collected. He shook the wanna-be P.I.'s hand like he was canvasing for votes. "Good morning. I'm Tucker Boyd. This is Angela Alexander. She had a late-night call and we fell asleep here. What's your name?"

The man blinked his eyes like hazard lights. He looked down. I dashed off to grab paper towels and sop up the brown mess. "I'll run out and get you another coffee." Shit. I felt like I did when I was sent to the principal's office in eleventh grade after Rosie and I cut class for a concert.

"Forget it," he said with a harsh tone and sneer, I imagined a bit like Robby's sadistic Marta. "I'm Neil. Here for my shift. You're the Angie I've heard about? I pictured you differently."

Okay, well, this first impression didn't go well. The door chimed again. In breezed Geneviève.

"Oh, hi, everyone. I see you two have met already. What are you doing here, Angela?"

"Hi Gen. Um, this is Tucker. Tucker, Geneviève."

Every day I grew more comfortable answering calls.

"Hello, North Yarmouth Grief and Support Line. This is Angela. What's your name?"

"Hey, it's me. I just got home and found your thermos of split pea soup on the counter like a queen without her subjects."

"Tucker, you're not supposed to call this line."

"You didn't answer your cell."

"I turn it off during my shift. The last thing some depressed person needs is my "Fly Me to the Moon" ringtone going off in the middle of their time."

"You can turn it to vibrate."

"I could, but I'm going to turn it off."

"Do you want your soup, cheesecake?"

"Yeah, I'm hungry. You don't mind bringing it?"

"No. I love you."

"Love you too."

Click.

Oh my god. He loves me.

"Hello, North Yarmouth Grief and Support Line. This is Angela. What's your name?"

"Help... I need... what's your name again?"

"Angela. If we get cut off, you can call back and ask for me. What's going on tonight? Can you tell me your name?"

"J... J... Janet."

"Janet, where are you?"

HONK HOOOOONNK

"Are you driving Janet? Can you pull over to talk? It's safer."

"No... I... oh god. I'm stuck in a p...p...parking lot on the toll way... I'm... I can't breathe.... I think I'm having a p... p... panic attack. I'm not sure... I never had one before."

"It's okay, Janet, I'm here. I'll stay with you."

"(Gasp, gasp) Thank you."

"Do you think you're having a physical medical emergency? Are you sick?"

"No.... panicked.... feel trapped in this... it's (gasp) terrible traffic... no trees... I need... trees! I feel disconnected (gasp gasp) like I'm hovering overhead."

"Janet, I'm going to help get you back into your body. You're not getting enough oxygen. Will you breathe with me? We'll do four slow breaths in and..."

"No. I can't! Just... help me!"

"Janet, what's your favorite color?"

"I... I don't know."

"What color are you wearing?"

"Green. I like green. Like the trees."

"Describe what you're wearing. What's the material? What style?"

"Umm. It's a cute, umm, pullover top. Rayon. Soft. Like, not bright, but... like sea green. Got it at Macy's two-for-one sale. Has like a drapey cowl collar. It's short, like... umm cropped..."

"That sounds really nice."

"It is."

RUUUUUMMMMM. KKKKKAAHHH.

"What was that Janet? Are you okay?"

"Motorbike! Clipped my side mirror. Oh, God (gasp gasp.) I know you'll have to answer other calls."

"No. Don't worry about it. I'll stay with you as long as you need. Can you see to drive okay?"

"Yes, I'm readjusting the mirror. Why isn't this traffic moving!"

"Janet, do you like music?"

"I love music."

"What's your favorite song?"

"I don't know. I can't... think..."

"Is there a song that helps you feel peaceful?"

"Yes."

"Good, what?"

"*Blowin' In The Wind*."

"Do you know the words? Would you like to sing it?"

"I want to (deep inhale) sing, but I'm shy. Umm... Not sure of all the words."

"That's okay, Janet. You can hum the parts you don't know. Would you like for me to sing with you?"

"Yes."

Janet started out softly, humming over the words she was unsure of. "How many years, hmm hmmm hum hum hum..." The tempo picked up along with her confidence. She ended with a glimmer of brightness in her voice. "I'm in my driveway now. I feel better. Thank you, Angela."

"I knew you could do it. Thank you for singing with me. You have a beautiful voice. Remember I'm here Tuesday and Wednesdays from 6:00 to midnight. Call me anytime."

"Thank you, bye."

"Bye."

Click.

"Hi, Angie. How's my favorite gemstone seller?" It was Geneviève calling.

"Great. I'm out for a run. Waiting to hear from a book distributer. It's frosty for fall. My bones are frozen and my cheeks Moulin Rouge rouged. How's that azurite and malachite crystal cluster working out for you?"

"I love it! It's sparkling up at me right now. It's supposed to alleviate worry, right?"

"I don't know. Maybe."

"I can't believe how fast things are moving…" Geneviève sounded excited for me.

"I know, right!" Things with Tucker were barreling forward like a locomotive.

"Yes, that's why I have to call an emergency meeting at the Center."

"What for?" My head did a 180 from Tucker to the talk line.

"The Finn-Pazernov family philanthropists want to move forward with funding the center. With you onboard, my confidence has rocketed. It's time for the board to clarify our mission. I hope you and Neil will get along when you get to know each other. You just caught him off guard."

"Oh, I see… the… okay… um… a meeting. When? Whoa!" I had Socrates with me and had to steer him away from the cute little Collie who was making goo-goo eyes at him.

"I know it's short notice, but is there any way you can make it tomorrow at 1:00? The Finn-Pazernovs are coming in at 3:00, so that will give us a few hours to draft our vision."

"Two hours isn't enough time. I suggest we meet by 10:00 and take a lunch break."

"See, this is why I need you. I'll tell everyone 10:00 and order in lunch. What are your dietary preferences?"

"Um, healthy. Salads. No meat."

I phoned Tucker. "I won't be able to see you until tomorrow night. I'm throwing you over for that guy Neil."

"Oh, I see how it is. I'll call Jack and cry on his shoulder."

Neil arrived a few seconds before me. He held the door open, and I had to duck under his arm like we were playing *London Bridge Is Falling Down*. In his other hand was a cup of coffee. I held my breath as his cup waivered. All we needed was a coffee spill to start the day out right.

"Good morning, Neil. How are you?"

His look said: *I wouldn't have had to come in a few hours earlier if it wasn't for you.* "Fine. You?" he said.

"I'm good, thanks. I'm excited about the meeting." And I was.

Being that I often run a tad late, the others were seated already. "*There* they are!" Geneviève announced, which punctuated our nearly tardy arrival. "Everyone, have a seat." She was dead serious. This was her opportunity to give to her community. My heart swelled by her goodness. "Angela, you've met Neil and Mandrel. This is my Sarah, my daughter, and Deena Cooper."

"Sarah! Finally, we meet!" She hugged me. "Deena, so nice to meet you." Our hands folded one over the other like a stack of cards. Her flesh radiated a loving warmth.

Mandrel, in an exceptionally tailored navy suit stood, wearing his height gently, and gave a warm stack-of-cards handshake, "Angela, it was sharp thinking to suggest more time for the meeting."

Then they all greeted Neil. Everyone seemed at ease with him, though his posture was stiff. I took it personally. Tucker told me not to worry about him. He said I'd win him over, but I didn't want to have to try to win him over. I couldn't get a clear read on the guy. Or maybe I had a clear read, which was in direct conflict with the social interaction around me. We're taught to trust our instincts. This is hard to do when the outer and inner conflict. Neil and I were seated next to each other. I smiled at him. He pressed his lips together and sipped his coffee.

Geneviève stood at the head of the long table with her hand over her heart like a proud mother giving the toast at an engagement party. "I'm thrilled and honored to have you all here as my team. I know that you all have lived your own dreams. This is *my* long-time dream.

"With a master's degree in sociology, same as Neil and Deena, I'm concerned about our society and relationship patterns, especially in a world knocked off its axis. I'm responding to the needs of humans, as I see it, for out-of-the-box avenues to talk and be supported. Traditional hotlines certainly help some people, but the foundation is biopolitical and violates the rights of many. The assumptions and foundation of what passes for mental health care worries me. I believe in choice in matters of life and death, which is what unities Mandrel, Angela, and me in our vision."

Deena and Neil studied me and Mandrel with curiosity. The vibe from Neil was sour. Since we met, Gen and I spent dozens of hours getting to know each other. We'd chat in the shop during lulls in business. I knew about Johnny and her daughter Sarah's recent miscarriage; she knew about Jack, Tucker, Madeleine, Henry, and my support for the right to die with dignity.

In graduate school, in between running a marathon and enjoying frequent sex, social outings, and thought-provoking dialogue with my healthy and eager young boyfriend, I interviewed people about their attitude and desires towards death. I know, the life of the party, right? At first, I was unnerved inquiring about death and regressed into nail biting, but with practice I became bold.

My fellow students, youthful, beautiful, brash, and buoyant, thought themselves invincible unless, like me, they'd experienced the loss of a loved one. Those who experienced a surprising or harrowing death were often eager to talk. Folks in the grips of grief or trauma avoided the topic, but others yearned to dialogue about their fears, hopes, frustrations, and concerns. I also turned to teachers and advisors who welcomed the conversation. My quest to understand how people dealt with their own death blossomed into my master's thesis.

The central focus of my paper regarded attitudes about self-deliverance: how to prevent non-rational suicide in people in temporary throes of a crisis that will pass, and support rational deliverance for those in permanent and progressive pain whose cost/benefit layout of life is in the deep, dark, and unrecoverable red. At the root of the research, I assessed the shame and blame often aimed at those who choose self-deliverance, (commonly called suicide) in the modern-day Western world. The topic is a contentious one for obvious reasons: we are losing a lot of souls who might have healed and thrived if nurtured, supported, and aided by managing the underlying or transitory causes of their hopelessness or illness. Survivors are usually gutted.

Attitudes toward suicide have varied through time, across cultures, religions, and philosophies. In large part however, the "S word" (suicide) carries a negative attribution bias. A common response when someone hears about a suicide – without understanding the life and conditions of the departed – is to jump-hop right to the conclusion that this death should have been *prevented,* someone failed to *listen,* and the person who choose to leave was *selfish.* My dear Madeleine, however, was not an egocentric degenerate. In her honor, I was pulled to challenge "S" stigma.

Thus, out of a protective post-mortem for Madeleine and others who came before and will follow, I threw myself into my project, *Suicide Isn't Selfish.* I became more assured using the "S word" when I learned to identify and discriminate between rational vs. non-rational suicide and to elucidate those differences to my interviewees. Irrational suicide might arise from a trauma that may well pass with time and support. Rational suicide refers to cases that are serious, incurable, and may involve unbearable pain. My search for answers informed my questions.

Is the practice in Western culture of judging intent and blaming the deceased without digging in deep and inquiring why self-deliverance has been around forever an acquired prejudice? Might deliverance be the sane, rational, humane choice in various and sundry circumstances?

Some philosophers argue that suicide is the most basic human right. If you can be forced to live against your will, then fundamental agency is denied you in your tenure on earth.

Activists who work to guarantee the choice to humans of when they die maintain that under acceptable circumstances, such as age, pain, illness, and irremediable suffering, the individual ought to be respected and supported in terminating their own life. Because life is good for one, it doesn't mean it is good for all. Because one has hope and possibility of improving their lot doesn't mean that everyone has that opportunity due to circumstances beyond their control.

Worries about physician-assisted death revolve around angst that the impoverished or disabled will be coerced to die against their wishes. The opposite seems to be true. There are many people who wish to be released from the body but are prevented from doing so. Furthermore, I discovered an increasing number of people that support an individual's right to make their own decisions rather than giving that power to doctors.

"My goodness, Angela, you've devoted your life to these issues!" Gen exclaimed when I told her about my thesis work.

"It's compelling. Driving provides benefits; however, some drivers kill through drunkenness, negligence, or accidents. Yet, automobiles are not outlawed. The sinister side of transportation is the focus of concern. We don't discard a valuable right for the minority who abuse it."

"The history of suicide fascinates me." Geneviève had done some thinking about this. "In the Roman Empire, suicide wasn't against the law. It was only forbidden to those accused of capital crimes, soldiers, and slaves because of the economic loss associated with their lives. I've never met anyone as committed to this issue as you. You ought to speak with Mandrel. His mother killed herself because of chronic pain. He believes she should have had the right to choose."

The spark to my fascination regarding death with dignity arose after Madeleine's suicide, which shadows me like an umbrella hat I cannot remove. Years later, my fervor was fueled by the death of grandpop Henry, my dad's daddy-o. My father and I both take after Henry: we are generous, convivial multi-taskers who set our sights high and strive step-by-step to reach the moon. The word "no" is a challenge to defy; our habits are set hard and steadily followed with joy and grit.

Phil and I have Henry's nose, lips, chin, forehead, and gumption. When grandpop faced a series of progressive ailments in his nineties - arthritis, a heart stent, and fluctuating blood pressure, which caused dizziness and accounted for three falls, his world became small and gloomy. He was in pain, isolated and bored. Grandpop, a first generation American, owned a series of gymnasiums along the Eastern Seaboard. He was adaptable as well as determined. He studied French cooking in his eighties and then knitting and crochet when his body demanded that he remain seated more than before. His living story took a turn after that third fall.

At ninety-four, he broke his hip and nose. He was hospitalized for a month, then bedridden at my parents' house, frail and vulnerable. He, and we, knew recovery was unfeasible. He resented being trapped in his wasting body, unable to change the situation. He panicked about what his future held and sobbed often because he felt like a burden. He did physical therapy but refused to take opiates. They made him nauseous, dizzy, and confused. He appealed to my father and I, "I want to die. Please help me leave this useless body. I'm in a living hell."

My father and I, Henry's power-of-attorneys for health, met with his doctor. There is no right to die law in our state. "Take care of him, keep his mind busy, and wait it out. Hope for a miracle."

Wait it out.

Hope for a miracle.

Is this the best we can do for an elder when their life has come to a painful and inevitable roadblock? According to Henry, *his* miracle would've been to leave his body without enduring more of the mess he was in because the right to die remains unchallenged. In some hospice programs, patients are given high doses of morphine to keep them comfortable, which is sometimes a means to end their lives. Many of the people I interviewed relived traumas of relatives either kept alive artificially against their wishes or involuntarily medicated to death.

Henry was outspoken about the lack of respect and consideration shown him in his final years. His doctor said perky things like *believe in yourself. Hang in there, Mr. Alexander. You have many good years left.* Grandpop, who didn't have any pain-free, independent *moments* left, flipped his physician the finger behind her back. "I'd like to shred her white coat."

My grandfather's incapacitation occurred while I was away at graduate school in England. When I hastened home after graduation, I found my once powerhouse, gym-going grandpa skeletal and sad, wasting away in an electronically operated hospital bed in my parents' cheerful living room. He took hold of my soft, fresh hand in his bony, feeble one. "Angela, I've been busy."

"Doing what, Henry?" I leaned in to hear every word he had to share.

"Starving myself. They won't let me out of this body. I have to find my own way."

Dear Henry died three months later. His unshaven cheeks were concave. He wore diapers, had a catheter and IV, and finally eligible for hospice, he refused morphine, of which he was terrified. Madeleine was twenty, Henry, ninety-four. Both deaths were disastrous and cruel as far as I was concerned. They'd have been better handled with choice. None of this sat right with me.

Henry divided his estate between me, my parents, uncles, and cousins. I was clear what I would do with my inheritance. While still mourning for my beloved grandfather, Rosemary showed me a Victorian house that was perfect for my Bean There, Done That bookstore. Henry would have approved of the pretty place and my pragmatic choice.

In the community center meeting, I didn't want to explain my personal history. Everyone has a storied past that informs them. I'm sure that Neil had beliefs and experiences that shaped his world. I wished Geneviève hadn't brought the topic up, but then, it is a central concept of ours.

"The argument for the right to die can be a slippy slide." Deena doodled circles on her paper.

"I think you're referring to the slippery slope," Mandrel added. "The Slip N' Slide was the highlight of summer when I was a kid. Man, a little water from the hose and whoosh, you went flying." Everyone laughed - even Neil. Mandrel can say anything and people like him.

"It's the continuum fallacy." I spoke up. "The death with dignity topic involves many questions. Is the act of allowing this human right going to lead to anarchy? Will people call it quits because they have a bad day?" I thought this subject might arise, but in the moment, I flushed.

Mandrel, undoubtedly thinking of his mother, said, "I'm with you, Angela. I think it's an important right. Slippery slope arguments usually don't pan out. The slippery slope I worry about is the continued restrictions of civil liberties that force people into lives of abject suffering. The Netherlands and Belgium legalized euthanasia in 2002. They retain a high respect for human life, whereas countries with lower morals overall oppose the right to die with dignity."

Deena didn't want to be left out. "I'm with you both, but there are so many ethical questions."

"If people get the right mental health care, suicides are prevented. In twenty years as a hospital social worker, this is my experience." Neil threw his credentials out as proof of his rightness.

Mandrel and I were both ready to respond. I used my inner mantra, *listen. Listen. Breathe.* Deena drew her circles bigger, darker, and faster. Gen intervened. "There is plenty to discuss here in future meetings. I'm glad we can respectfully do so. The question for today is *what kind of organization is ours?* My vision is for a talk line, really a *listen* line, not a suicide line."

"An expression line," I offered. Deena laughed. Mandrel put his hand on my shoulder and nodded.

As the hours wore on, we staggered and lurched our way into a mission statement that satisfied everyone. North Yarmouth Talk

Line and Community Support Center presents a new paradigm in which people from all walks of life can call to be listened to with anonymity, without judgment, advice, or intervention. Within six months of establishing the talk line, a community support center would be launched to offer a comforting, safe space for people to spend time in.

Learning from the downfall of the Automat Restaurants, the homeless would be expected to shower at the shelter first. No fragrances would be allowed, as exposure to topical fragrances can trigger allergies, skin sensitivities, and cause harm. People could come to cry, talk, laugh, celebrate, play games, talk, rest, get space from their homes or jobs, and socialize.

Throughout the meeting, I occasionally imagined what Tucker would say. Though I trust my own intelligence and instincts, my boyfriend, by virtue of his wise and warm ways, had woven his way into being my hero and role model. I phoned him at the lunch break.

"Hi Tucker."

"Cheesecake! Have you achieved world peace yet?"

"Mayor, I don't even have peace with Neil."

"Oh no, what happened?"

I gave him the thirty-second rehash.

"Well, you know, it's like that with some people. You can't please everyone. The rest of the group sounds wonderful. Try to enjoy the afternoon and hurry home afterwards. I miss you."

After lunch, our spirits lifted. We brainstormed ideas for the center. Hammocks. Healthy food. Birthday celebrations for those who don't have family. A game and music night. A communal bulletin-board. Geneviève was attuned to the zeitgeist. Communities are growing scarce. People are desperate by escalating world problems and increased isolation in their lives. The particulars were nebulous, but nevertheless, our whole group was enthused by the mission.

By the time the Finn-Pazernovs showed up, we presented a strong, united front. Fran Finn-Pazernov wondered, "Are you trying to be all things to all people with too big a scope." *Nope,* we said. *It's time for this. All we need is love* - and a big generous check from some like-minded philanthropists. And that is exactly what we got once the donors received a written proposal.

The night of the philanthropists and community do-gooders meeting, I rushed home and beat the mayor at *Jeopardy!*. The next night, the talk line was buzzing all night. A few callers stood out.

"Hello, North Yarmouth Grief and Support Line. This is Angela. What's your name?"

"Bob. How ya doing, Angela?"

"I'm doing well, Bob. What's going on tonight?"

"Well…. HEY! ZACH! GET DOWN OFFA THERE. LEAVE YOUR SISTER ALONE! (Sigh) I'm not doing so well, Angela. My wife died and left me with two kids. I love 'em, I'm a good dad, but they're driving me crazy. Between work and parenting, I got no down time. No time to grieve. HEY! WHAT DID I SAY?"

"It sounds like you really have your hands full, Bob. How long has it been since she died?"

"Four months."

"What was your wife's name?"

"Her name was Angela, too, believe it or not."

"What was she like? Would you like to talk about her?"

"She was like the breeze, Angela. Gentle, unexpected, ruffled me up from time to time. (Laughs) She was the world's best mother. She loved these two. I don't know what we're going to do."

"She sounds wonderful. It's… quite a loss. How did you meet?"

"At a gas station. She was pumping gas and I gave my number. We went out that weekend, got married two months later. That was it. We just knew. That was… hmm… 'Bout ten years ago."

"How old are your kids, Bob?"

"Zachery's nine, Joey, that's my girl, Joey's gonna be eight. Hmm. She looks just like her mom."

"I'm sorry for your loss, Bob."

"T'aint your fault."

"I'm not apologizing; I'm just empathetic for you and your family... So ... do you have anyone that can help watch the kids so you can have a little breathing space for yourself?"

"I've been too embarrassed to ask, ya know. Hmm. I got a friend who offered. Maybe I should take her up on it? What do you think?"

"I don't know your friend. Do you trust her with your kids?"

"Yeah, yeah, I do."

"Let me know how that goes, Bob. I'm here Tuesdays and Wednesdays from 6:00 p.m. until midnight. Call me anytime."

"I will do, Angela. I will do."

Click.

The next night, Wednesday, was a bit slower. The evening kicked off with this call:

"Hello, North Yarmouth Grief and Support Line. This is Angela. What's your name?"

"Hi."

"Hi. Who's this?"

"Zach."

"How old are you, Zach?"

"Nine."

"What's going on tonight, Zack?"

"I miss my mom."

"Was her name Angela?"

"Yes."

"Do you want to tell me about her?"

"Yes."

"Okay."

"She was the best mom in the whole world. We played baseball. She could hit really good. We did art and flew kites. She made me do my homework before I watched TV. She was just nice and pretty."

"Who's with you tonight, Zach?"

"Carrie. She's my dad's friend. She's babysitting."

"Do you like Carrie?"

"Yeah! She's totally cool."

"You don't have to, but just because I'm concerned about you, a minor calling on your own, would you mind if I talk to her for a sec?"

'No. CARRIE! SOMEONE'S ON THE PHONE FOR YOU."

"Hello?"

"Hi Carrie. This is Angela from the North Yarmouth Grief and Support Talk Line. Zach just gave me a call. I think he just needed to talk a little bit, but I wanted to make sure everything's okay over there."

"Zach, are we good tonight, buddy?"

"Yeah. I just wanted to tell Angela about my mom like my dad does."

"Oh."

"I'm glad everything's okay. Do you want to put Zach back on?"

"Sure. Zach, here..."

"Hi."

"Zach, how's your dad doing?"

"He's pretty good. He went to the movies tonight. He says he needs to get away sometimes."

"Do you want to talk more about your mom?"

"No. Not tonight. Maybe another time?"

"Sure, Zach. I'm here Tuesdays and Wednesdays from 6:00 p.m. until midnight. Call me anytime."

"Okay, bye."

"Bye."

Click.

On Wednesday nights, Neil's shifts jut up against mine. Seeing him every week in passing remained the low point of my week. I tried to understand him and be kind, but I didn't like him, and I'm usually easygoing with everyone. As I ended my time, Neil arrived with coffee piping hot and a tight-lipped smile. When he heard me sing or have a honeyed human interaction, his disapproving disposition left me self-conscious and clammy. His energy put me on red alert.

It wasn't the fact that Neil opposed the right to die with dignity that put me on edge. I've met many wonderful people who clash with the concept, and others who worry about how right to die will function or fail. Some, like Deena, are concerned about the Slippy Slide. I could not find a sweet spot with Neil. He embodied an arrogant resentment to the world. I did not know why.

A month after the grant meeting, I had a typical bevy of calls. Nothing earth-shattering, no threats of wrist slitting, just the usual array of people calling for some loving support.

"Hello, North Yarmouth Grief and Support Line. This is Angela. What's your name?"

"Pam."

"Hey, Pam, what's going on tonight?"

"I've never… I never called a talk line before."

"Everyone needs a listening ear sometimes. What's happening?"

"My cat died. I can't stop crying. I'm a basket case. I'm crying more for my cat than for people. I think there's something wrong with me."

"There's nothing wrong with you, Pam. I get a lot of calls from people grieving their pets."

"Really?"

"Uh-huh. Just got off the phone with someone whose turtle, King Solomon, died."

"That's a good name for a turtle."

"I think so too."

"I can't talk to my husband or my friends about it. They think I should be over it already."

"How long has it been?"

"Two weeks."

"Would you like to tell me about your cat?"

"I got her when I was in college fifteen years ago. A friend's cat had kittens. This one was always jumping up on my lap or nipping at my heels. I had to take her. She chose me. She was beautiful and playful, a Manx."

"I had a Manx too!"

"Then you know how amazing they are! She'd hop around like a bunny, without her tail. She was my favorite part of every day."

"What was her name?"

"Mookie. She was mischievous and spooky; used to hide under the covers and pop out to play -- a real sense of humor."

"Oh, yeah, they do. How was she spooky."

"Her eyes glowed in the dark. Used to scare Mike, my husband, when he was my boyfriend."

"That's a big loss -- your favorite part of everyday."

"Yeah, I don't know what I'm going to do. Have you ever lost a pet?"

"Two cats and a dog."

"What did you do?"

"Same thing you're doing. I mourned, remembered the good times. Put together a video. I went running... a lot. I still miss my babies."

"The Manx is the new one?"

"She was the last one. Jasper."

"Oh, I'm sorry. That's a nice name. How did you get it?"

"I love gems. I always take names of stones and minerals for my pets."

"That's a great idea! I might do that! I mean.... IF I ever get another one."

"It's okay. You don't have to decide now. It's only been two weeks."

"Right. Only two weeks. I feel a little better from talking."

"I'm here on Tuesdays and Wednesdays from 6:00 p.m. to midnight, call me anytime."

"Thanks. Bye."

"Good night."

Click.

"Hello, North Yarmouth Grief and Support Line. I'm Angela, what's your name?"

"Hey, it's Robby."

"Hey, Robby, how's it going this week?"

"Shitty. Leg still hurts. Now my parents got the bright idea to put me on crappy antidepressants. I've heard teens kill themselves from those. They gain weight, lose their sex drive, and have you read those side effects? That shit would be worse than how I feel now. I don't understand. Why do they want to medicate me? It's natural that I'm upset. I haven't been able to ski for a month, lost my spot on the basketball team..."

"It's been a month already?"

"Yeah. Time flies when you're hobbling around in a cast. NOT."

"What's the outlook for healing?"

"Ummm-don't know. It hurts a little less, but still keeps me from sleeping well. Supposed to heal. Hopefully. Not sure. I miss the endorphins from working out."

"I know what you mean, I run like clockwork every day."

"What would you do if they wanted to put you on freakin' crappy medication that has nothing to do with the problem?"

"Robby, you know I can't give medical advice."

"But..."

"I wouldn't want to take it. Can you walk yet to start getting back some natural endorphins?"

"I walk, but just not much yet, you know? I tried doing some sit ups and pull ups this week, but I don't want to overdo. It made me feel worse, so I got upset, and they start in with the medication talk again."

"Oh, shoot. I hate to hear that you're dealing with this. You sound stronger than last week though."

"I do?"

"To me you do. How do you feel?"

"Stronger. I started writing like you suggested."

"That's great. Keep doing your best with the physical therapy. Let me know what happens, okay?"

"Yeah, you here tomorrow? I gotta figure something out."

"I'll be here."

"Okay Angela, I'll call you then."

Click.

"Hello, this is the North Yarmouth Grief and Support Line. My name is Angela, what's your name?"

"Bill."

"What's going on for you tonight, Bill?"

"My dog... di...died. Abbott. He was my best friend."

"I'm so sorry, Bill. You want to tell me about him?"

"He went with me everywhere. Shepherd-Collie mix. Good boy. Loved fishing, hiking, bicycling, came with me to the store, everywhere. You must think it is odd, people dealing with real problems, and I call crying about my dog."

"I get a lot of calls about pets, Bill. You're the third one tonight."

"Any other dogs?"

"Not tonight. Turtle and a cat."

"Well, I'll be. (Cries) He was just such a good boy. Who am I going to go fishing with now? (Cries again) Hang on a minute..."

(Muffled) "I'm on the phone, Jill." (Muffled)

"My daughter came by, Angela. She said she'd like to try fishing with me." (Cries)

Silence.

"Okay, Bill. That's sweet of her. I hope you have a good time. I'm here Tuesdays and Wednesdays from 6:00 p.m. to midnight. Call me anytime."

(Cries) "Thank you."

Click.

My shift flew by as it usually does when calls are steady.

"Hi, Neil."

"Good evening, Angela."

"How was your day?"

"It was fine. Yours?" His habit was to communicate with me through the minimum number of words he could get away with. On occasion I pushed the envelope though. Tucker said I expect everyone to act with my warm nature. He did too, but he said I am naïve about it. And so, I am.

"Neil, do you ever get calls from people whose pets have died?" I gathered my things as I spoke.

"Yeah. Sometimes. You would think someone would have something better to do than call a talk line about their dog. As if we don't have enough real problems in the world."

Whoa. Does he understand life, love, and grief at all? Why does Geneviève have him here? Then I prepped myself -- *Anything you say will set him off. Anything.* Beginnings of five sentences shot through mind. *Have you ever had a pet? Do you have any sensitivity at all? What do you actually say to people who are hurting? Why are you so smug? What the hell happened to you in your life?* I was a complete, devastated wreck when sweet Jasper died. Imagine if I had been unlucky enough to talk to Neil about my devastation!

Instead of any of that, I said, "Have a good night," and ran to my car.

In the grant proposal Geneviève and I wrote, it stipulated that after a month of a successful talk line, which included being on call twelve hours a day to start, employing an 800 exchange to forward our calls, and serving an underserved population, we would have the go-ahead to proceed with opening the community support center. The opening day of the center was on a Sunday.

Geneviève and I worked on the wording for the welcome plaque:

Age, money, parenthood, fine clothes, a fancy house, or positions of power; none of these things elevates a person in wisdom or increases loving kindness. The ability to listen, empathize, meet responsibilities and extend the golden rule to elders, the infirm, friends, family, and strangers, deeply, in an ongoing way, are priceless qualities that can't be measured in dollars, appearance, or French fashions. When did the idea arise that one needs to be happy all the time or that happiness is a symptom of maladjustment? Joy and tragedy arrive unmasked and unannounced. The North

Yarmouth Community Support Center is here as a buoy in the turbulent sea of life.

Mandrel said, "Job well done!"

Deena said, "I love it!"

Neil said, "Don't you think it's over most people's head who come here?"

Tucker showed up on opening day with flowers and his band, Tyrone, Angelo, and Claudia. Rosemary, in vintage culottes, was with Ronny, her beau of the day. Jared and some childhood friends came to show support. A few of my customers and booksellers popped in for a moment but stayed for a whole set by Tucker's band. Mandrel's wife and four little girls, each a head taller than the next, brightened the room. Deena was solo, and Sarah and Ben arrived with great news – they were pregnant again. Neil's good-looking teen son Sam was aloof. A modern-day James Dean.

Forty members of the community came by. We hoped for more but expected less. They gobbled up burritos and fruit salad. The band played "Wade in the Water," Molly Drake's, "How the Wild Wind Blows," Kate Melua's "Nine Million Bicycles," "Thirsty Boots" by Eric Andersen, Leonard Cohen's "Chelsea Hotel" and "Suzanne," and ended with "Girl From The North Country" by Dylan. Tucker never played down to a crowd. Everyone left with brochures and a buzz of good energy.

I woke up the next morning and threw up. I asked Gen to give me the week off from the talk line until I got better. On Thursday morning, recovered, I was ready for a run when the phone rang.

"Angela. Hi, it's Geneviève."

" Geneviève! Hi. Congratulations on Sarah and Ben's pregnancy. The photos you sent are wonderful. How are they doing?"

"We're all fine. I'll be here for another week. I'll call and catch up with you in a few days."

"Why are you calling on this line? Is something wrong?"

"Yes. I'm not sure if you're aware of the contentiousness between callers and Neil the night you were out sick."

"No. What happened?"

"Well, you have very different styles, to say the least. I've been inundated with complaints about Neil, to which he has responded with a complaint about you."

"About me? What did I do? What's everyone saying?"

"I got, let's see, onetwothreefourfivesixseven... eight... eight complaints saying that Neil had no place answering calls for a talk line, they miss you, and suggested that you give staff trainings."

"Oh, my. I'm sorry for the drama."

"And then Neil said you told a teenager not to take his medication. So, let me ask you a few questions. I hate to do this, I know you, and I'm not worried about it. Just bear with me."

"Sure."

"Okay, um, number one, are you telling people not to take medications?"

"No. But shouldn't his anonymity be protected?"

"Tell me without using names, or make up a name, although I know who it is. He calls me, too."

"All right. You know Robby is one of the most levelheaded people I know, is a star high school athlete whose leg was shattered in an accident. His struggle with loss and pain is totally natural. His parents want him to take antidepressants, to which he's opposed and distraught about. When asked what he should do, I told him I couldn't give medical advice. When asked directly if I would want to take them under the same situation, I said 'no.' What's the next question?"

"What are your interactions like when you change shifts? Based on past complaints, his dour demeanor, and now this outcry, I have to figure out how I can let him go."

"It's always uncomfortable. I'm friendly. He is angry, gruff, and non-empathetic. I'm scared of him and feel compassion at the same time. If I called in, I wouldn't want to talk to him."

"Thank you for your honesty."

"You're welcome. The third question?"

"Would you be willing to co-teach the next six-week volunteer training course coming up in January?"

"Yes. I'd love to, Geneviève. Let me check with Tucker about the schedule first. I'll get back to you in a few days."

"Thank you, Angela. Keep up the good work. Call me if you need anything."

"Will do. Enjoy North Carolina. Bye. Hey, Geneviève?"

"Yes?"

"Can you get the transcripts from Neil's calls?"

"Great idea. I should have thought of that. Give me a few minutes. I'll email you."

Among the transcripts I recognized some of the callers.

"Hi. This is Neil. Whatsyrname?"

"Isn't this the North Yarmouth Grief Call Line?"

"Yep. Sure is. Whatsyrname?"

"I want to talk to Angela."

"She's not here."

"It's her Wednesday shift. I just talked to her last week, and she told me to call back tonight. Where is she?"

"I don't know, sick or something. Why are you calling every week? Are you suicidal?"

"I'm upset, man. Having a hard time. I shattered my leg. My parents want to put me on antidepressants."

"Okay, so why don't you go on them?"

"Because they... that's not what Angela would say."

"What did she say?"

"She wouldn't want to go on them either and agreed they wouldn't fix.... Hey, know what? I don't like your tone, man. What's your name again?"

"Neil."

"Congratulations, Nei-ill. I call a crisis line and you make me feel like shit. Way to go."

"Sounds like you need more help than I can give you."

"F--- You, man! I need to talk to Angela!"

Click.

"Hi, this Is Neil. Whatsyrname?"

"I'd rather not give my name."

"Suit yourself."

"You can call me Donna."

"All right. Whatsup?"

"I'm in a lot of pain and it makes everything hard. Everything. Just getting up in the morning, eating, walking, moving... People don't realize how good they have it if they're not in serious pain."

"Sounds like you need morphine."

"What! Morphine? What are you...? I called to get support. I feel really overwhelmed sometimes because I don't have a break from this pain!"

"Have you prayed?"

"I'm secular, Neil. I don't think it's appropriate for you to talk about religion with me. Is there someone else I can talk to? I need someone to talk to."

"Call back. Maybe you'll get someone else."

Click.

"Hi. This is Neil. Whatsyrname?"

"It's me. We just talked. I'm calling back. I want to talk to someone else."

"Well, you got me again."

"Put me on with your supervisor."

"There's no supervisor on at night. You can call back Monday through Friday 8:00 - 4:00."

"What was your name?"

"Still is. Neil."

"Well, Neil, I don't know why you're doing this job. Maybe you're a good person, but you have ruined my night."

"Sounds like it was already bad, DONNA. You need to find faith and be saved."

"Oh, my..."

Click.

"Hi. This is Neil. Whatsyrname?"

"Zach. Is Angela there?"

"Nope."

"But it's Wednesday."

"Look, kid, she's not here."

"When's she coming back?"

"I don't know, Zach. Why are you calling a grief call line? Don't you have parents?"

"My mom died, and my dad is at a movie."

"I can call protective services for ya. Get you put in foster care. What's your name and number?"

Click.

I still wasn't feeling great, but I wanted to get back on my shift to undo the damage done, so I had my next call line shifts redirected to my cell phone.

"Hello. North Yarmouth Grief and Support Call Line. This is Angela. What's your name?"

"Hey, you're back. Just wanted to make sure. Your replacement is a real jerk."

"What's going on tonight, Robby?"

"They made me start taking those pills last week after I got off the phone from yelling at that TOOL head. I've thrown up every day since then. This shit's making me crazy, and I feel fuzzy headed. I'll call and let you know how I'm doing next week. I gotta go throw up again."

Click.

"Hello. North Yarmouth Grief and Support Call Line. This is Angela. What's your name?"

"Hi, Ang, it's Bob..."

"...And Zach..."

"We just wanted to make sure that you were back. Your support has gotten our family through some hard times... "

"I'm sorry for any stress you've been caused..."

"We're fine, Ang. Going out to toss a basketball around. Your colleague was ready to farm Zach out to foster care."

"It won't happen again."

"We'll talk to you another time. Glad to have you back."

Click.

"Hello. North Yarmouth Grief and Support Line. This is Angela. What's your..."

"You bitch! Geneviève just called and let me go. I've known her for two years. I helped her plan the talk line. What the fuck did you say?"

"Neil, I'm going to hang up now, and I ask that you not call me again."

Click.

7.
THE ANDEAN CONDOR

My normal life swept me up for the next week. The store was crowded like Harrods at Christmas. The smell of coffee and cherry pie cozied up the place. Jonah Dunn gave a comedic talk and signed books. On Living Story Night we hosted a Syrian woman who sought asylum in the states. Tucker and I saw *Durango* off Broadway and visited Brynn and Michael. The trip was perfect; we four formed an enchanting family unit. Tuck and I headed back Tuesday afternoon in time for my shift. I walked into the community center peaceful as a bear going to hibernate.

"Hello. North Yarmouth Grief and Support Line. This is Angela. What's your name?"

"Hey..."

"Robby! How are you? Haven't heard from you in weeks. I've been worried."

"They want to put me in the cuckoo's nest. I can't eat, am sped up, have cotton mouth and stomachaches, shit doesn't help the pain in my leg, doesn't give me back my life. They keep changing meds. Up and down like a seesaw. I get sick, they say 'take more' or 'try another.' I was fine until I fell. They say, 'try harder,' as if the problem is me and not that they're using me as a damn chemical lab experiment. They've known me all my life. It's like they never knew me. I'm the star quarterback, top student, and good son. How can they not know me all of a sudden?"

"Oh, no, Robby. Does your therapist understand? Can she help? I'm here to listen, but I feel limited in what I can do."

"No, she's not a therapist; she's a quack. She's crazy. She says, 'medication will fix you.' Has no idea how humans work."

(Muffled)

"Robert..."

(Muffled)

""Gotta go, Angela. Can't you help me somehow? Think of something. I don't want to be put in a loony bin."

Click.

"Hello. North Yarmouth Grief and..."

Loud music blares *"You better look behind you cause there I'm gonna be. I'll be standing in the shadows..."*

Click.

"Hello."

"Tucker, it's me."

"Babe, what's wrong? I'll be done with this shoot in an hour."

"Do you have a few minutes now? I'll make it quick."

"Yeah, yeah, sure. What's wrong?"

"Robby called. He doesn't have anyone trustworthy in his life. He said they want to put him in the hospital. I feel so powerless; all I can do is listen. Then Neil called blaring that music..."

"Enough is enough. We'll get a restraining order on him this week. That guy is nuts."

"I need to figure out how to help Robby. Then I need a break. Can we get out of town? Maybe to the beach? I need to sit and watch the gulls by the ocean or drink in the beauty of the earth."

"Say no more. I started planning a trip that includes your choice from the *Jeopardy!* win. You can also quit the call line or take a break. Nothing is worth your health and well-being."

"No. Neil's not going to scare me away. I won't let him. Ooh... the phone is ringing. Bye, babe."

Click.

❦

Our surprise destination before our holiday landing place was to the rich coast, Costa Rica. Tucker had assiduously planned this unexpected first leg. He knew I hadn't seen my ex-pat parents in nearly two years, and he was profoundly keen to meet them.

"Turnabout is fair play. You met my parents; it's time I meet yours." As we arrived at the airport he plopped the itinerary in my hand with the pomp and circumstance of bestowing a diploma upon a graduate.

"What *exactly* should I bring?" I had yelled as I threw clothes asunder from closet and drawers like a cat digging through a garden.

"Layers!" he laughed, so pleased with himself for pulling off a surprise excursion.

I was excited to see my family and have them meet my blues-singing boy, but I'm so-so on the place my parents live. They love the beach and after Henry died, they need to relax. Me? I needed my fix of the bright lights of the city, the hum and flow of creativity: museums, gallery openings, plays, theatre, and the wonders of the world. I was young and had fuel to burn.

Little did I know that a new world would be opened to me by traveling with Tucker. You have not seen Costa Rica until you see it through the eyes of a bird and nature photographer. The day we arrived, he ticked off ten species of birds and butterflies on his must-see list, the second one while I introduced him to my mother. "Mariana, this is Tucker Boyd. Tucker, my mom."

She, who had vowed off make-up when she left the Cape for retirement, wore a deep satin plum lipstick. My dad Phil wore a Beatles *White Album* tee-shirt to impress Tucker.

"Mariana." Tucker took her by her shoulders and swiveled her ninety degrees to the east. "Do you see up there?"

"Where?"

"There" he said as he pointed just past my mother's head into a mass of twigs on the overhead tree, "is a White-whiskered Puffbird. Do you hear it? It has a wispy cry. This little cutie hunts by a watch-and-wait technique. It sits motionless before darting to catch its prey... Oooohhh. There it goes!"

"Ahhhh," my mother swooned. She turned at me and winked, signaling that this was my first boyfriend to impress her.

After showing Tucker the different varieties of Costa Rican lettuce at the grocery store, the four of us donned our boots for a hike. My father knows all the best places to go, but he's a novice when it comes to nature.

Tucker pointed to a Darkened Rusty Clearwing Butterfly, "Their wings lack scales, so the clear chitinous membrane between the visible veins appears see-through."

"Oh, I know that one," my mom gleamed proudly. "This is the mariposa espejitos, the butterfly with little mirrors."

"*Muy buena y que es eso?*" Tucker said as he tiptoed towards it. The bird had seemed to appear from out of nowhere. "The majestic Great Green Macaw. Notice how its tail is laid out on the palm front it's perched on." He lifted a small camera from his jacket pocket and clicked away.

"I know this one." My father grabbed Tucker by his arm, eager to impress him. "There is a Red-headed Barbet."

"Shhh." Tucker approached cautiously so as to not scare him away. "It's a male. The males have a red head, an orange to yellow breast, and white belly. A white collar separates the head from the olive green back. The amount of color on the throat and chest varies among the subspecies."

"Oh, my goodness, it's absolutely beautiful. Get a good shot of that one, Tucker. I'd love to frame that for the living room," my mother always had decorating on her mind.

We trekked and birdwatched for a few more hours before the daily downpour. "Come, let's retreat to a warm home and some hot tea," my mother, a wonderful hostess, enjoined us. While the Boyds had titillated me with their music and company, my parents wowed Tucker with their vast knowledge of literature and history. Watching them interact together was like enjoying the sense of harmonious and beautiful proportion and balance in Paul Gauguin's *Landscape at Pont Aven.* Everything blended just so. The conversation flowed. Mariana glowed.

Every night they read passages from *The Correspondence of Gustave Flaubert & George Sand.* The letters span from 1863 to 1876. Sand and Flaubert tenderly, frankly, and poetically talk of their lives and the world. As a bookseller, I recommend this book to many customers of literature and history. No serious reader has ever been disappointed. On our last night, I was distressed when Tucker's knees bounced up and down. I hoped my parents weren't boring him.

"Phil, may I interest you in catching a bit of night air, just the two of us?"

"I'd be honored."

Upon being left alone, my mother, never one to be at a loss for words, inquired, "Is he the one?"

"Mom, you know I don't believe in the fairy tale of the prince."

She raised her eyebrows. "If that man is not your magical person, I don't know who will be."

Up until I was twenty-three, I went along with aspects of societal thinking that are so prevalent they are often taken for granted, without question. I love kids, and before I fully matured, I assumed I would have a large biological family. I was everyone's go-to person to take care of their kids. "The Child Whisperer," they called me. When I became an entrepreneur, I realized I did not want to have biological children or get married. I'd turned away several proposals from men who wanted to father my children. Concerned about global resources and potential earthly disasters, I expected to adopt older children later in my life. Last, but certainly not least, after the frightful deaths of Madeleine and Henry, I could not justify bringing a child unasked into a world without the guaranteed right to opt out if it becomes intolerable.

"Have you told him where you stand about children?" My mother cleaned up like she did everything, with precision and grace. Plates lined up her arm, food bits slid into the compost, and napkins went in the wash bin. She crossed and uncrossed one knee over the other.

"Yes."

"And?"

"He says he wants to be with me. Socrates is his boy. If I want to have children, biological or not, it will all be good with him."

"Are you blind, Angela? He's dazzling."

"That lipstick is gorgeous on you." I hugged her.

"I wonder what he's doing out there with your father for so long?"

Just then, the men appeared in the doorway. My father slapped Tucker on the back.

"You two look like you have a secret." I was dying to know what they talked about on their own.

"Tucker here is desperate to see a Resplendent Quetzal. Tomorrow we're going to drive to the forest to find him this most beautiful bird." Dad was always good with a quick cover.

"The quetzal is worshipped as a god. Its iridescent green and red plumage was sought after like precious stones. It has a yellow beak and multi-colored tail that is up to sixty-five centimeters long. It would really make my day to see this sublime bird."

"As you wish, Tucker. As you wish."

Weary from our flight from Costa Rica to Cusco, Peru, Tucker and I unpacked at an ornate hotel that used to be a monastery. I meticulously arranged doll-sized travel bottles of shampoo and lotion in the bathroom. "You do realize we're only here for two nights, right?" Tucker teased.

"Yes, sir, mayor."

"Ang, what do you say that we unfeignedly defile the ancient vibes of asceticism and chastity here while we reach our acclimatization line?" The acclimatization line is the level you want to reach regarding the high altitude before trekking the Inca Trail.

"Sounds good, mayor!"

An alarm woke us at 4:30 a.m., after having achieved our defiling goals and then falling into a deep time zone-zagged sleep the night before. There was barely enough light outside to see the budding sunrise lifting on the horizon. Tucker kissed me softly.

"I had that dream again," he said. "The one where I'm free-falling off the cliff at Hightower, tumbling head over feet, arms akimbo. This time there were three birds circling so close, their feathers brushed lightly against my skin like a pfooopf blowing the puff off a dandelion. I had wings like propellers, the size of a handball court, sewn together between my shoulder blades."

"Oh, you blessed man. I wish I had more flying dreams. Tell me more on the bus. I'll write it down in case you want to use it for lyrics." I pulled him up, threw him his pants, "catch," and lined his brush with toothpaste. "C'mon, babe. Let's get on that first coach."

We gobbled cold leftovers: grilled cauliflower, artichoke, and mushroom frittata we'd saved from dinner the night before as we pulled on our clothes and boots and assembled our gear.

I travel with a light cross-shoulder satchel to carry water, money, ID, and trail mix, which I carried for both of us. Tucker was outfitted for a safari. In addition to carrying a backpack with ponchos, hats, and sweaters, he had his twelve magnification binoculars that allowed him to see a wide field of view, something like 380 feet at 1000 yards. Many times, he explained to me how refracting telescopes worked, but my head is made for literature, not birding equipment. Also looped over his neck was a weather proof single lens digital camera that had a quick autofocus at a high ISO, which is useful in animal photography, according to my birdman.

"All you're missing is your conga drum, Tuck."

"And my piano, but this will do." He gleamed at his camera as though he had just struck gold.

At 5:30 a.m. sharp a cheery turquoise bus pulled up half a block from the Aguas Calientes train station. A line of clone-like bright buses filled with international tourists who converged to hike the Andes. The vehicles groaned and purred over Hiram Bingham Road. On the bus, Tucker, a languages whiz, led people in English, Spanish, French and Chinese to cheer Bingham, the American explorer who unveiled the Inca City to the world in 1911. Japanese, Indian, and Danish travelers caught on and joined in too.

Our bus pulled up to the door of the archeological site. "Cheers again, Hiram Bingham," Tucker toasted with an imaginary champagne flute lifted into the air. "*Acclimations, Skål, Salud, Prost, Na zdravje,* Hiram Bingham," we heard behind us, fists of all colors lifted in salute. At 6:00 a.m. sharp the doors opened. After a passport check and a long list of rules, in we went.

We'd watched videos of the area, but nothing prepared us for the majesty of Machu Picchu in person - towering mountains, a maze of green terraces, crisp air, and dancing, shifting clouds as far as our eyes could see. After several hours of hiking, we were well above those clouds. The steps were a workout even for Tucker and me, who were fit and athletic.

"This place is just unbelievable! Look at these views!" I outstretched my arms like a hawk, and tilted my head back, misty eyes overlooked a verdant landscape.

We caught clear glimpses through flawless crystal skies as the atmosphere changed as quickly as a puff of air. Big plops of cool rain fell on my face. The layers of ledges were higher than Zeus spread out like an ocean of fertility, generous in its gorgeousness, slippery surfaces, and uneven ground. "It's my dream," Tucker gushed. "I feel free here. Like I'm flying."

We trekked on, admiring the interlocking walls of the city and exalting in the brilliance of the Incan architects. We had decided in advance to hike out to the Incan bridge, which is one of the entryways into Machu Picchu.

"Look Tucker, it's a secret back entrance into the place."

This trail is free to hike, but we had to sign in. As we ascended, we peered down at steep drops without the luxury of guardrails to protect us.

"Wow, that is a straight drop off the cliff. Don't think you're a bird and try to fly, Tucker. Now that I found you, I don't ever want to be without you."

"I feel the same way, cheesecake. There's the trail. Can you see the bridge ahead and the gate beyond? Be careful, there's only a wire to hang on to. This is a stunning and insane place."

We explored and braved sketchy ledges for eight hours, climbing up and down stairs. We followed a series of one way signs and sometimes lost sight of Machu Picchu. The idea is to avoid a human traffic jam, so the signs directed us in ways that didn't always seem convenient.

"It's just like life, right, Angie? We follow the yellow brick road."

We ran into Bodil and Bernardus, a couple from Amsterdam we had met while admiring the paintings in our hotel. "Hallo! We're going to hike down and explore the city. Have you been?"

I lightly elbowed Tucker to stop him from saying, "Bean There, Done That," but I myself answered, much to Tucker's delight, "no, we haven't been there."

"So, see that?" Bernardus pointed. "It's the city gate. We're going to walk down and through. Join us?"

"Yes, of course," Tucker accepted. "This is amazing! We're in somebody's house right now. Windows, shelves, cabinets. Whoa." He adjusted the camera lens and clicked away. He staged creative shots of our Dutch friends, Bernardus snapped us, and a Slovakian couple took the four of us together with a prized background behind.

Then we six followed the trail to the sacred plaza, Inti Watana. The sundial. Andíl, who had visited this site, before explained, "The sacred rock is the trailhead to Huayna Picchu. Do you know what Huayna Picchu means? Shh, not you, Silverstein," Andíl addressed his quiet partner. After waiting to a count of eight, he continued, "Huayna Picchu means small or young mountain and Machu Picchu means big or old mountain. Can you imagine hiking up that?"

"Yes! Let's do it!" The mayor was always ready for a new adventure.

We entered an agriculture area to learn about farming in the terraces. The Inca made and built houses or temples in the terraces with dirt from ten miles away because the mountains are all rock. They built the retaining walls with the rock from these mountains. Three feet of imported dirt stood below us, and sand beneath that, then the rock, and finally, the natural earth.

"Wild animals including wildcats and pumas would try to get into the city at nighttime, so the fortresses were secured to keep them out," Tucker read from a guidebook. "This is a royal house. It has a bathroom. You only see double doorways going into royal homes or temples. As nice as this stonework is, it's even better in the temples where the stones are perfectly shaped."

Andíl, something of an expert on the area added, "When Hiram Bingham found Machu Picchu in 1911, it was overgrown with five hundred years of jungle. Archeologists are slowly removing the trees and restoring the terraces. This path was part of the original Incan trail that leads to the sun gate. Puerta del sol. It's uphill the entire way, with stairs that disappear into the jungle. Tucker, would you like to lead the way?"

Tucker was transfixed on some llamas on the grass. "Hang on, man, just a few more shots."

"Catch up with us then, mate." Bodil and Bernardus took up the lead, then Andíl and Silverstein, and bringing up the rear, Tucker and me. Not once did I think about all my responsibilities at home: my shop, co-running the call line community center, or the contentiousness from Neil.

When we reached the Temple of the Sun, the rain stopped. The lowering sun gleamed and twinkled off our heads, flickering in brilliance with alternating shadows. We all looked up.

"There they are! The Andean Condors! Angela, the condors!" Tucker lifted me up and twirled me around there at the top of this world wonder. Then he ran round and hugged our comrades. "The condors. The condors. Here in the Andes!" With wingspans of eleven feet, these spectacular black vultures accessorized with white plumage on the neck and wings glided and soared in concentric circles, catching the updraft currents in the sky. Each loop around sent a thrill through our bodies, like a roller coaster that suddenly lifts off into the air.

"Don't you want to take some photographs?" Bodil interrupted Tucker's reverie, returning him back to earth just long enough to catalyze him into action.

"Yes, of course. I do! Thank you, Bodil!" He hugged her again.

"Stop hugging people, man, and point your camera. This may be a once-in-a-lifetime opportunity," Silverstein nudged Tuck.

I was thrilled for him. Here he was in his element. *Did he ever think that after Sheba died, he would find any glimmer of happiness again? How crazy life is with its ups and downs, peaks and valleys, which we could quite literally see standing on the top of this mountain.*

The condors, the largest flying animal in the world, rarely flapped; they sailed through the sky over our heads. They are the stuff that myths are made of. After their flight migrated to the east, and Tucker caught the last clear shots he could of them, we sat, stunned, taking it all in.

"We better go before dark." Bernardus, the first on his feet, prompted our group to move.

"Sure. We'll bring up the rear again." Tucker jumped up too. As the others began the descent, Tucker bent down, I thought to tie his bootlace. "Angela." He reached into his pocket and took out a round gem-cut natural amethyst on a silver chain. Kneeling on his right knee, he did not tie his lace; he held the necklace up to me. "Will you marry me?"

Bodil, Bernardus, Andíl, Silverstein, and some twenty other tourists all fixated on me, breathless, and not just because of the thin air. "Yes, Tucker, my love. As witnessed by the majestic Andean Condors, Kuntur, messenger of the gods, and these good people of Peru, I love you with my whole heart and soul and want to spend every moment of my life as your partner."

"I asked your father in Costa Rica. He gave us his full blessing."

I popped my fist on his shoulder. I *knew* they were up to something!

"I am an official wedding officiant," Bodil offered. "Would you like to have a ceremony here?"

"Now?" Tucker and I exchanged excited glances.

"*Ja.*"

My *anam cara* and I, our souls aflame, answered. "*Ja.* Yes. Please."

Gathered on a peak of heaven on earth as the sun sparked from gold to orange to red and the condors, or maid of honor and best man, spun overhead in spirals of approval, we promised to take each other as husband and wife, for better or worse, until death do us part.

Our international friends jubilantly jumped up and down, congratulating us in seven languages in the auspicious Temple of the Sun. I never dreamt I'd meet and marry such a magical man as Tucker Boyd. We were literally and figuratively on top of the world.

8.
WELCOME HOME

Tucker and I went off the grid for the rest of our trip. *Our honeymoon*. It was a joyous departure from our wonderful but pressurized daily life. Our sights were saturated with Central and South American blues, browns, beiges, and reds. High on love, we listened more acutely to the squeaks, chirps and caws of the birds and chugs, whistles, and whirs of natural life. We tuned into each other's breath, posture, and gestures undisturbed by beeping of mindless demands on our time. *How can this be our life!* We were condor kites bobbing in the effervescent wind.

We ruefully reconnected to electronics on the concourse from the plane to the baggage claim carousel. Tucker had a few messages about jobs, gigs for the band, invites to parties, and a call from his mother. I, on the other hand, was inundated with calls and messages.

"Hello, Geneviève?"

"Hi, welcome back. I hope you had a good trip."

"Yes! Can't wait to tell you about it! What's going on?"

"Someone threw a rock through the community center glass."

I fell back to earth.

"Who would do this?"

"The police think it's Neil. There's a warrant for his arrest."

"What!"

"They are patrolling your house and bookstore. He's livid about being let go from the center. I tried to reach you all week. You ought to find a temporary place to stay until they find him."

"Look, our bags are here, Geneviève. Let me call you right back."

Tucker pulled our packs off the carousel, unaware of the conversation I just had. "I love you, Mrs. Alexander-Boyd. I can't wait to start our forever life together." He picked me up and spun me like a Condor circle. "Oh, no, what happened? Bad news?"

We slept on Rosemary's couch for a week. Same spot where we met. Tucker had three days of shoots in the city but didn't want to leave me until Neil was found. The incident made the local news. After the telecast, everyone but those of us involved forget about it. My mood, which should have been soaring high after I wed the love of my life in Peru, had a wash of worry, a grey-black undertone that had me trembling to the bone.

I did my next shift from my cellphone in Rosemary's apartment. I wasn't the only one who felt a dark downturn. The talk line saw a two hundred percent uptick. We urgently needed to find caring, competent volunteers. Tucker offered to temporarily take some shifts, and since Geneviève knew and trusted him, she put him on. The callers reminded us that we were not alone in this dark night.

"Hello. North Yarmouth Grief and Support Line. This is Angela. What's your name?"

"Darnell."

"What's going on tonight, Darnell?"

"I don't feel well."

"I'm sorry to hear that. What's wrong?"

"What's NOT wrong? The country's gone to hell in a handbasket. I just was a pallbearer carrying the casket of my best friend. Shot by a policeman. Why? For nothing. Best man I've ever known. Close from kindergarten until we were grown. Boom. Now he's dead. I wish it was me instead."

"Darnell, I've heard a lot of life stories, and I'm at a loss for what to say. I'm here to listen and... *sigh*... I'm so sorry he had to die."

"Thanks, Angela. People don't listen to each other. We cry out and nothing changes."

"Would you like to tell me about your friend?"

"Yeah. Um, yeah, I would. He was a good, no GREAT teacher. Taught English. He loved those pretty words. Always telling me this book is better than the movie. I like the movies better, ya know? (Laughs) Always going the extra distance for this student or that. Spending every penny of his money on supplies. Never expecting any prize, just gave his all, ya know? We'd go hiking, bike riding, bowling, just hang out in the weekends. Anytime I needed a shout out, Thomas was there. Now no one's there. No one cares. They killed me when they shot him." (Cries)

"What a tragic loss. He sounds like he was an astonishing friend."

"He really was. To the end."

"I wish I could do more, Darnell. Is there anyone else you can talk to? You might need more support than me, but I'm always here to listen."

"Not many. Thomas, he was my man."

"What do you do for work?"

"I'm a teacher too. Biology."

"Science guy. I admire that."

"You're a gem, Angela. Thank you for listening."

"I'm here Tuesday and Wednesday nights from 6:00 to midnight. Call me anytime."

"I will definitely do that."

Click.

"Hello. North Yarmouth Grief and Support Call Line. This is Angela. What's your name?"

"Chris."

"Hi, Chris, what's going on tonight?"

"They're messing up our water. Killing our people. I can't wrap my mind around it. I feel powerless. Trying to protect our land. I feel

numb. Tired. I don't know what to do. Don't know what to do. Do...
not... know... what... to... do... Sorry. Probably shouldn't have called."

Click.

"Hello..."

"Hi, Angie. It's me. Sorry to phone you on the call line. Just really quick, did you feed Socrates?"

"Yes."

"Okay, babe. Love you. Have a good night."

"Bye."

Click.

For the next month, due to various and sundry world events, calls flooded in beyond the capacity of the few of us to handle. The community center window was repaired. Mandrel, Geneviève, and I did the trainings. Tucker turned down jobs so he could help out and chauffer me everywhere until they found Neil. We found some eager psychology interns to volunteer. I ran the training.

"Carla, Rashid, Yusef, Manny, Paul, Quinn, Bai, Lara, John, Jon, Dalisa, Adio and Lydia, thank you all for coming in tonight. As you can hear, the phones are ringing off the hook. Remember, we don't give our own political comments - this is a talk line. We listen. You might not agree with a caller's viewpoint. I can tell you it will be hard but do your best to use the tools we went over in the training. People process in different ways: grief, anger, shock, and denial. If you need me, signal me or come over and tap me. People are devastated tonight by this election."

Lara muffled a cry.

"Are you going to be okay, Lara? You can go home if you want."

"I'm okay. I want to be here."

"Okay, have at it. Good luck."

"Hello, North Yarmouth Grief and Support Line. This is Rashid. What's your name?"

"Hello, North Yarmouth Grief and Support Line. This is Quinn..."

"Hello, North Yarmouth..."

"I'm depressed... worried about my green card..."

"I'm Muslim and worried about what's going to happen to Muslims in America..."

"I'm black. I'm shocked by what's going on, I don't want to live in this country anymore..."

"I work for a labor union. This is a nightmare..."

"Country's f-ed!!"

"I'm disabled. I'm worried about how I will live if entitlements are cut..."

"It doesn't seem real. What does this mean for my healthcare?"

"Hi. I'm Riz. My wife and I disagree politically. We're like strangers on a train now. I don't see our marriage making it with the changing political climate in our world."

"I'm Holly. My husband and I disagree on everything now. It's like we're not even in the same reality. We don't share values; our relationship is like a lobster headed towards a pot of boil."

Click.

"Hello, North Yarmouth Grief and Support Line. This is Angela. What's your name?"

"Hi. It's Nonny. I know it's a busy night. Do you have a few minutes?"

"Of course, Nonny. You want to hear "Lullaby" by Cris Williamson?"

"Please."

I sang it tenderly as though she was a newborn I was putting to sleep. I heard Nonny take what was likely the first full breath of the day.

"Thank you. Goodnight."

Click.

"Angela, what was that about?"

"Manny, there's a three-year-old dying of leukemia. Sometimes I sing lullabies. It's just something I do. You're not expected to."

"Ummm. That's so sweet that you sing to the little girl."

"To her mother." *And in my mind to Lena, Madeleine's mom.*

"Excuse me, Manny. Hello, North Yarmouth Grief and Support Line. This is Angela..."

"Hi, it's Robby."

"Robby. What's going on? It sounds so loud where you are."

"They put me in the hospital, Angie."

"ANGELA – I NEED YOU OVER HERE! THIS GUY IS REALLY SUICIDAL. I DON'T KNOW WHAT TO DO."

"Robby. We have a crisis over here. Hang on a minute..."

Tucker and I found joy in being together through the stressful slog of self-imposed semi-isolation as we waited for the police to find Neil. We installed cameras on the house, put up an iron gate and stayed home more. I worried for Neil and his family. Socrates growled and tugged at our tee-shirts to try to get us to take him the dog park to see his girlfriends and chase frisbees. One night after we played catch late with Socrates in the yard to calm him and tire him out, a buzz came at the gate. *11:30 p.m.? My mouth was dry.*

"Who is it?" I snapped. Socrates slept through the commotion. Some help he was.

"It's me. Geneviève."

Tucker hopped out of bed into one pants leg, then the other, and ran to let her in. She was in sweats, her hair like a rat's nest in a top ponytail. I'd never seen her disheveled like this.

"Hi, Angela, Tucker. The police found Neil."

"Did they arrest him?"

"No. He's dead."

A sharp knife-like jab pierced me in the lungs.

"Someone murdered Neil?" Tucker looked like he was trying to multiply pi by pi.

"Overdose. Likely suicide. It'll take four to six weeks for the autopsy results."

"I'm so sorry." I hung my head.

"Angela, whatever the results, stop blaming yourself. Whatever Neil's problems were, they had nothing to do with you or me. He was different when I met him. He changed over the years. It happened so slowly I didn't see it. After his behavior, I had to let him go from the talk line. I asked if there was anything I could do to help, but he was hostile. Sam said he was on a lot of medication."

"Oh, man, it's so sad for him and his family." Tucker sat and put his hand to his chin, as he does. His pinky finger jut out as it does, which drew Geneviève's attention to his hand. She grabbed it.

"What's this? Are you two married?"

I pulled out the ring I wore on a necklace.

"When did this happen?"

"In Peru."

"Congratulations! Were you going to keep it a secret?"

"We were waiting for some resolution with Neil. Didn't feel like celebrating."

"I understand, but you have to live your life. When we move past this tragedy, I'd like to throw a reception at the center for you. The community loves good news. I can't believe YOU'RE MARRIED!" Her shriek awakened Socrates, who yapped and danced around her.

"There's my phone. I'm still on shift. Hello, North Yarmouth Grief and Support Line. This is Angela..." I stepped from the kitchen into the living room.

"Did you hang up on me last week?"

"Robby, of course not; I said I'd be right back. I'm director of the center now. I had to triage. There was someone suicidal on another line. When I came back you were gone."

"I was brought to a psych ward."

"Oh, no! What happened there?"

"They didn't find reason to admit me. You know why? Because I'm fine. It's my folks who need help. They still have me on crap medication. Switched meds so many times I'm dizzy, or maybe that's just one of the nifty side effects. Does nothing positive for me, doesn't fix my shattered leg, makes me feel scary and weird, but at least this one doesn't make me throw up."

"How much pain are you in this week?"

"A lot. A little less than last week. Physical therapy helps, but it's hitting me hard that I'm not ever going to be able to play ball professionally, which has been my dream since I was a kid. I don't know what I'm going to do, Angela. First thing I need is to get my dad off my back and get off these fucking meds. Will you talk to him?"

"You know I can't. I'm here to listen to you, but I can't interfere. Three months until you turn eighteen and can legally make your own decisions."

"Maybe. Until I can support myself, I'm still at his mercy."

"Maybe you can find a therapist or social worker who can help you more hands-on."

"Yeah, right. (Snorts) I called the numbers you gave me. You don't realize how bad the system is until you're caught in it."

"Did you write this week?"

"Yes. I'd love to read you a short story sometime."

"Would it be possible for you to call earlier tomorrow? The later it is, the busier the lines are."

"Yeah, I'll call earlier, but Angela?"

"Yes?"

"I need you to interfere. Now. I don't care what the rules are."

"Let me figure something out, Robby."

"Okay. Please. Do something. I'll call tomorrow."

"Call back in fifteen minutes."

"It'll be after midnight."

"Call back. I'll pick up."

Click.

I called the exchange. "Hi, this is Angela. Keep forwarding me calls for the next half hour."

In the kitchen, Tucker played Jackson Browne's "Linda Paloma" for Geneviève. A beautiful song, it has an upbeat Mariachi sound with vihuela guitar, guitarrón, violin, and harp. Tucker strummed his guitar as fast as hummingbirds fly and added in all the little Mariachi whoops and hollers with the help of Socrates, who had a grand time howling along with company over since he missed his playmates. I loved the song but couldn't wait for it to be over.

"Excuse me. I'm sorry to interrupt. Geneviève. I have to do something about Robby. I can't just sit by knowing he's being mistreated. He's a minor but he's begging me to help. He turns eighteen in a few months, but the damage will be done. He's going to call in fifteen minutes."

"His coach is supportive, right?"

"Extremely."

"I'm free tomorrow. Ask him if we can meet him with his coach. We're a community. I don't feel right sitting by either. You've talked to him for a long time."

9.
KEIRAN AND TIPPLER, MAINE

"Hello, North Yarmouth Grief and Support Line. This is..."

"Is this Angela?"

"Yes, it is, who's this?"

"Angela, you don't know me. My name is Kieran O'Shannessy."

"Huuuh, Kieran O'Shannessy? I thought you died!"

"No, that was my father, Kieran. I'm Kieran Junior."

"Oh, Kieran, how's your mother, Mary Rose? I haven't heard from her in a week."

"That's why I'm calling. I'm sorry to let you know Ma passed away last Tuesday. The last thing she talked about was calling you to have you sing her a lullaby."

"I'm so sorry for your loss, Kieran. Your mother was a great woman."

"Thank you. We... I... thought so."

"How are you doing? Would you like to talk about it?"

"No... thank you... on behalf of my Ma, I'd like to invite you to her memorial service. It's at half past three, next week Sunday, at the Big Brown Church at Cotters Point in Maine. Ma requested that we invite you. It'd be a real honor if you can attend, but I realize it's a lot to ask."

"Oh, my, up in Maine. Well, I'm off that Sunday. I'll ask my husband to come along. Maybe we can all drive together? Mary Rose talked so much about you. She was incredibly special to me."

"We... I... loved her very much. She was loved, you know."

"Yes. I know. She knew."

"It's just. I'm divorced, kids are grown, and the economy has been tough for my business."

"Kieran, I understand. It's hard to juggle everything."

"Angela, I didn't sing to her every night. We... didn't have that kind of relationship. Our family is very grateful to you. Ma was happiest Tuesdays and Wednesdays when she could call you."

"Kieran, she knew you loved her. I'm glad I could help."

"Angela, (sniff, sniff, swallow) it's just that I miss her so much (sniff.)."

"I'm here, Kieran. What can I do for you?"

"Would you.... can you (sniff).... sing something to me?"

"Yes, I can do that, Kieran. What would you like to hear?"

"Do you know "Fly Me to The Moon"?"

"'Yes. Great choice."

I closed my eyes and sang the first verse from my heart to Kieran's. I closed my eyes and lost track of time and space. Tucker entered with pea soup he made me. I peeked at him and motioned for him to put it down. He kissed me on the forehead, then sat, and sang silently alone.

"Thank you, Angela. I see why you were soothing to my Ma.

"Tucker texted me back. We'd be honored to go with you, Kieran."

"Meet at the center at half past eight, then?"

"Sure. We'll see you then."

Click.

Sunday was our day to spend together, but Tucker and I believed in our mission of support for those left alone. Ten minutes into the drive, Kieran was too emotional to be behind the wheel.

"Kieran, pull over. Tucker will drive."

Tucker maneuvered down unfamiliar roads as Kieran nervously fingered his father's old rosary. "I don't know why I carry this," he said. "Neither he nor I were religious men in the least." The semi-deflated wheels of his pale aqua Chevy Impala crunched on twigs scattered by the storm. A blanket of fog broken by insolent sunlight fell in horizontal silver stripes across the meadows and settled in on the misty harlequin green grass.

"Round the bend there," Kieran pointed out to Tucker, "past the Peekaboo Pool Hall."

The building sat defiantly across from the old schoolhouse. "The peeling paint on those strict red doors was refreshed each season by my Da, who dipped a four-inch steely brush into a rusty paint can he kept safe in the cellar. Da took on this task every three months so the kids would have a cheerful welcome. He did this until he was too ill to leave his house, though no one asked, seemed to care, or ever gave him a wee nod of thanks. Ma stayed home and took care of us lot."

There, a few feet past a quad of fuzzy baby goslings nosing Pinocchio beaks into the topsoil, scavenging for breakfast, stood the pastor, the man Kieran was searching for: straight and slender, mousy brown hair flopped down on his forehead as wind blew chilly gusts across Tippler, Maine.

A mile past the pastor a tired old lighthouse survived, now defunct, unable to blink its large eye steadily into the dark night. "Slow down now. See this signal house? The memory of its light burns in my imagination. I see Da, his salty rugged aura, strobing out to sea and returning handsomely back to meet me. Ma, of course, is there too, faithfully bringing up the rear."

"Morning, Father, *dia duit.*" Kieran called out. "This here's Pastor McNeil. Walt, as my father called him. He's legendary to us Irish folk in these parts."

"Dia duit, Kieran. A sad morning it is, lad."

"Tis," our friend sniffed a bit. The men slapped each other on the back, softly like a preschooler patting a drum. "*Me comrádaí* here are Tucker and Angela. They are my life rafts today."

"Thanks for coming." The pastor lifted his hat to us and then excused himself to get ready for the service. Kieran gave us a little background. "Walter McNeal, Da, and my Uncle Whelan all grew up together when Tippler's tiny town was tinier still, population four hundred and ninety-eight. Now, we are ten times that and still a community tight enough to recognize most folks at the grocery and hardware, though a newcomer might sneak in and slip away unnoticed.

"This coast reminds me of Da. I'd constantly question this righteous patron of salt sea, fisherman of quahog, littleneck, cherrystone and steamer clams; cockles, scallops, mussels, haddock, lobster, cod, trout, alewife, halibut, bluefish and smelt he caught in reedy water; no matter my question, his answer was always: *the sea.* Ninety-nine times out of a hundred he was right.

"'Walk on the sand; it will soothe you, boyo. The water is wise. Listen well to it. Wake with the sunrise in silence. Watch the sun set with a friend. You will find your answers there, Kieran.'

"The pastor was a regular visitor of Da's. To me, it was always, 'Yes Sir, Father McNeil.' I kept this man at a distance out of awe, fear, and high regard. The town chatterboxes swear up and down to this very day that Father McNeil has an illegitimate son in Portland who is the spitting image of his high school girlfriend. We may never know the truth, not that it matters to me."

The congregation arrived in their Sunday best. The women dabbed at their eyes with handkerchiefs. The men blew their noses.

"Should we head over there now?" I wondered.

"Ay." He finished his story as we walked. "The McNeil and MacAuley families emigrated from Ireland, landed in New York and quickly made their way up to the striking miracle that is Maine. The boys, fast friends since they were four, were living parallel lives until, as budding men, they came to a fork in the road where Walter chose god and Kieran and Whelan chose cod."

Tucker laughed. "That is a good line. The rhyme. Did you just make that up now?"

"No. It's just what happened. Other than the wild crash of the surf, charming dive bars, roadside stands, cafes that served lobster rolls and fresh oysters, everything was buttoned up in this corner of Maine. I knew I didn't want to stay in teeny, tiny Tippler for long.

"I worked as a courier at sixteen. I flew from Paris, Oslo, Madrid, and more. You could take the boy out of Tippler but couldn't take Tippler out of the boy. As my job took me around the globe, I'd look at my reflection in dirty mirrors in stinky airport loos and feel guilty that Ma was lonely back in Tippler. After Da passed, I tried to make it up to her. My girl Marta in Dusseldorf put up with my comings and goings as no other woman would, but I moved back for Ma."

A smattering of townsfolk gathered for the service. "I expected a much bigger crowd. Right sad to think that so few will miss Ma in this town where she lived with such generosity and grace."

Tucker and I each took Kieran by an elbow and walked him to the service site. Father McNeil heaved a sigh, opened his bible and read a few passages, none of which I recognized, heathen that I am. The second-to-last verse he recited was Psalm 23, "The Lord is my shepherd; I shall not want. He maketh me to lie down in green pastures; he leadeth me beside the still waters."

"My folks weren't people of the scriptures, but they would've liked the part about the water," Kieran told Tucker. His cry was the bark of one unused to weeping. Tucker held Kieran up at that point. McNeil closed his book. The cozy crowd made small talk about Mary Rose, condolences swirled, and Mrs. Donovan invited all round to gather at her house after lunch.

We strolled up the high road in Tippler to get something to eat. The toasty and briny olfactory burn of The Flap Jack Factory hit us first. The neon sign is of a fisherman catching pancakes. "They serve pancakes all day, short golden-brown stacks with crunchy hash browns, white and moist on the inside, or medium stacks of sweet cheese or boysenberry jam filled flapjacks with bass, trout, or cod on the side. Da had convinced Marvin to add a Fishermen's Catch of the Day Special, and even after Marvin died, the tradition stuck."

"I'm starving. In we go," Tucker said as he pulled us inside.

Inside, the percussion of tintinnabulation was intoxicating. We studied the green chalk board. There it was on the top right side, *Fisherman's Catch.* Just beneath, a photo of Kieran Sr. Chalked to the left was a drawing of the red school door with a pink heart on it. It read, "Thank you, Kieran, we love ya and miss ya."

Kieran noticed a figure hunched over, back to the crowd, at the triangle-shaped corner table. It was the pastor. He lifted his chin from his Dr. Brown's Cream Soda and motioned us over. "Have a seat, Kieran. Angela. Tucker," he said in more of a question than a statement. "That's your Da's seat," he pointed to the round plastic cushioned dirty tangerine swivel chair. Kieran inhaled deeply. When we sat down, waitress Noreen came by with a pad, but didn't look at it.

"Fisherman's Catch?" Her smile was so lovely we could see it pierce through Kieran.

He nodded.

"It's on the house. For everyone."

"Thank you so much," Tucker and I spoke in unison.

Kieran turned back to the pastor to thank him for his service and lifetime of friendship with his family. The staunch man, stalwart, pillar of his community was gushing like a geyser; his tears streamed freely down his face and splashed onto his flapjacks.

"Father…," Kieran began.

The pastor took Kieran's hand in his. "Call me Walt."

"All right, Father, I will." We all laughed.

"Don't be a stranger. This is still your home. Come back and see us…" his words trailed off as he took out a handkerchief and blew into it, using up every dry corner.

"I've nothing here to come home to anymore, Walt."

Noreen set down our plates of pancakes stacked up like a lighthouse into the sky. The Fisherman's Catch of the Day circled the cakes.

"The door, Kieran."

"What?"

"Who's going to paint the red door if not for you? It needs painting every three months. You can stay with me if you want, no strings attached." Kieran nodded. Noreen warmly squeezed his shoulder, leaned in and whispered, "Fisherman's Catch of the day, every day, special for you."

Tucker and I were moved by Kieran's vulnerability and the goodness of Walt. The rugged beauty of the Maine cliffs made an impression on both of us, but more so on Tucker.

"If I ever die, scatter my ashes here, will ya, Angela?"

"As you wish, Tucker."

"Where do you want to be scattered?"

"Here too, if you are. Beyond that, I've never given it a thought."

We hurried back for a gathering at the center that night. Sunday nights were special. We celebrated birthdays and anniversaries of those in our community and lit candles on the death day of their dearly departed. There was no religion in our doings, just love. On Sundays, Tucker, and his band, Tyrone, Angelo, and Claudia played a concert and took requests. If one or the other couldn't make it, those that could improvised without them. There were days when Tucker came on his own. He was the holy man of the moment, always ready to lift someone's spirit.

On Monday, Tucker went to see his parents and do some work in New York. I'd have gone with him, but I was still breaking in new volunteer trainees at the talk line.

"Hello, North Yarmouth Grief and Support Call Line. This is Angela. What's your name?"

"Taur."

"Spell it."

"T A U R."

"Oh, just like it sounds."

"It's a nickname for Taurus. They say I'm stubborn like a bull."

"What's going on tonight, Taur?"

"Sometimes I feel like I don't want to be here anymore."

"Do you want to tell me about it?"

"I'm sick of the direction things are going. People are divided and divisive, and now... I'm sort of a whistleblower at work, which has opened a new world of opposition."

"Sort of?"

"I am. I saw a doctor do something that seriously harmed a patient. I reported it. Now I think I'm going to get fired."

"What do you do?"

"Nurse. Now, how can I do my job if I can't speak up, huh? How could I live with myself? I don't want to stand silently by."

"Wow, That's a tough situation. You made my night by being that strong person doing the right thing. I'm sorry it may cost you. That's real, I know. I get a lot of calls from people in your situation."

"It seems common, huh?"

"It does to me from my own life and from working the talk line."

"Angela, every time I get up on my feet and stand my ground, I get knocked back down."

"That reminds me of that Tom Petty song, 'I Won't Back Down.'" I began to sing it. Taur joined in. We shared a rousting round, fists pumping in the air.

"Thanks, Angela. I'll call back. When are you here?"

"Tuesdays and Wednesdays from 6:00 to midnight."

"I'm going home to put that song on. I'm worried about my job."

"Call me anytime."

Click.

"Angela, why do you sing on so many of your calls? Isn't that unprofessional?"

"By whose standards, Manny? We're dealing with human beings here. Music is universal. It touches people. I often suggest they spend time in nature, exercise, eat well, do artwork, write, sing, help others. We're having an advanced training in December. You're welcome to join us."

"I'll think about it."

"Okay, right now, let's answer some phones."

"Hello, North Yarmouth Grief and Support Talk Line. This is Angela. What's your name?"

"Robby. Just checking in."

"Hey Rob! How are ya?"

"Better than last week, but I'm still in sick shock and mourning my old life. It sucks."

"That's totally understandable."

"I have a little less pain thanks to the massage therapy. That was a great suggestion, by the way. After talking to Coach, my folks agreed to taper me off the medicine, see how it goes."

"You stood your ground and look at you!"

"Thanks to you and Geneviève. Stuff made me feel like killing myself. And the best thing that happened is some freshmen have asked me to coach them. It makes me feel a little useful."

"That's incredible, Robby! I'm so happy to hear that."

"Yeah, so, I'm headed over there now, so I'll read you the story another time."

"I'd like that. Tonight's not good anyway, I have to..."

"Triage?"

"Exactly. We've been getting a lot of despairing calls lately."

"You go sing to 'em, Angela. I'll go coach. I'll call tomorrow. I need to talk."

"Okay, Robby."

"Angela?"

"Yes?"

"You're as pretty as I thought you'd be. It was a pleasure to meet you."

"Same, Robby. Hang in there, okay?"

"I will. Bye."

Click.

"Hello. North Yarmouth Grief and Support Line. This is Manny. What's your name?"

"Carmen."

"What's going on tonight, Carmen?"

"My landlords are trying to raise the rent again, which is against the law, but they're bullies. They know I need a roof over my kids' heads. I just want to give up sometimes. I'm tired."

"I'm sorry, Carmen. Have you been able to get legal help?"

"No, but my cousin, he knows how to deal with this. He's going to help. Since Archie died, I have to do everything on my own. People say they'll help, but they get busy. I stand my ground alone."

"I know how hard it can be. I'm a single parent too. You sound like a great, protective mother. I commend you for standing your ground."

"That reminds me of that Tom Petty song."

"'I Won't Back Down'?"

Manny and Carmen sang a few lines of the song together.

"No, I won't back down.... Thank you, Manny."

"Thank you, Carmen. I'm here Tuesdays 6:00 to midnight. Sundays, noon to 4:00. Call anytime."

"I will."

Click.

"What's this, Manny? Did I hear you singing with someone?"

"Shut up, Angela."

"Okay, I'm sure it will never happen again."

Geneviève and Sarah surged through the front door. "Angie? Manny? Are you on calls or can you come out here?" They were bundled in hats, scarves, and peacoats with only pink noses showing. Sarah held a protective mittened hand over her belly, which had grown greatly since I last saw her. She walked in baby first, Sarah second. Manny and I knew what the news was.

"The autopsy results came back early. They found six medications in his system - three antidepressants, two anxiety medications, and sleeping pills."

"Suicide?" Manny asked the obvious. He had never met Neil.

"Looks like it." Sarah removed her mittens and blew hot air on her fingers. I brought everyone a cup of tea. The four of us sat dazed.

"I failed. I could help everyone else but him. In my store, the call line, community center, or in life. I have a warm hug and silent wisdom for them all, but I could not see the divine in Neil."

"Angela, stop doing this to yourself. It's not your fault. Neil had a lifetime of abuse and overmedication. Don't make this about you. He was nasty to you. You tried. I saw it."

"I saw it too." Sarah wrapped her cold white fingers around the mug. "He wasn't all that nice to me or Ben either."

"I'm going to Brooklyn to be with Tucker. I'm sorry for all the trouble I caused here. That rock was meant for me. That glass was my heart."

Geneviève stood up. "I let him go. It was a bad situation. We're going to have a memorial next Sunday at the center. Ask Tucker if the band can come to play. Neil's son Sam will be here."

"Will do."

10.

TEN KILOS ON

The next four years thrust forward as they do for two imaginative, productive people in love. I managed my shop through a roller coaster of economic turns. People still flocked to Bean There to share their living stories, more so because of the hardships in the world. They stayed to buy books. I initiated more online business with schools and programs for underprivileged families.

Encouraged by my internet expansion, Tucker launched *Home Sweet Home Staging*, a virtual business, so he could work from home or while traveling. Our mutual ardor adventure made globetrotting a regular event, even with all the responsibilities at home. We backpacked through Europe several times, hitting some usual suspects: Barcelona, Amsterdam, London, Paris, Rome, Venice, Budapest, Prague, Vienna, Stockholm, Copenhagen, and more, along with sweet smaller spots, including Meiringen, Switzerland; Assisi, Italy; Racha, Georgia; Buçaco Forest, Portugal; and Rovaniemi, Finland. In Japan, we saw the deer at Nara and Buddhist Temple in Kyoto.

The green *Jeopardy!* board was filled with travel destinations for years to come, including a post-retirement stay in Italy to become fluent in Italian – someday far off in the future. Tucker crafted a stirring portfolio of international birds in flight. I led him to homes of Chopin, Monet, Beethoven, and Kafka. Our priority was to get to know locals in each locale we visited through an organization dedicated to world peace through cultural exchange. We formed a network of musicians and intellectuals worldwide, including up the West Coast in America. We accommodated them, and they returned the gesture.

In Prague, we met Anna, who hosted us for three days. We walked to her childhood homes, schools, church, outdoor markets, hangouts, and nature areas. Her tours were woven within her life narrative, which flowed out easily and passionately to our eager ears. Anna shared intricate, personal details about the Velvet Revolution, which ended over forty years of communist rule in Czechoslovakia and ushered in a Parliamentary Republic. Her story, told through the eyes of the teenager she'd been at the time of the revolution, included details of her participation in the historic International Student Day. Through her story we learned details of the long effects the changes had on her contemporaries and country. Mutual hosting gave our trips meaning.

Geneviève made me vice president of the community center, which was daunting because it had taken a year for the community to warm to her vision. The idea was for people to get to know neighbors and community during good times and bad, to lend a hand to others when possible, and to have a community couch to sit on if one felt isolated, adrift, in need, or simply chatty. It wasn't a pub, counseling center, state agency, church, book club, dance class, or meet up group. Our rules were simple: no politics, religion, disrespect, or ads. Due to the fragmentation of society, Geneviève wanted to invent a new (old) way of coming together.

Tucker and his band Ten Kilos On donated their time to play some evenings and weekends. This helped warm the place up like a crackling fire on a cold winter's night. Birthday parties, birth announcements, and memorials became popular at the center. A large bulletin board connected people with others in need in a more real way than online communities. Sometimes people came to meet dates there in a safe space, or just kibbitz on a couch with others.

The band took their name from a song Tucker wrote. For the recording they hired a bagpipe player who blew the pipes at the end of each line, accenting the words "long," "upon," "gone."

TEN KILOS ON

The eve stretched loooong,
Our feet blistered and weary,
We were petered out,
Our spirits dreary.

We came upooon a quaint abode
As ten more kilos, we pushed; we strode
And found this peaceful place to lay our heads,
To sleep and dream from safe in bed.

Breakfast was chai and adzuki beans.
We were rich in love, though slight in means.
Many times, when we reach road's end,
Hope appears around the bend.

On days when darkness tempers our cheer,
We remember when life led us here.
To a quaint abode ten kilos on,
At a moment when all hope was goooone.

Paolo Paradis, the electric jazz-blues fusion star known for his shredding chops, invited Tucker to sit in with his band *Paolo Paradis and the Psithurism Paupers* in Brooklyn, whenever Tucker could make it. My exultant blues boy had a full and satiating dance card. He was elated.

Our relationship deepened in delicious ways. I danced out Shakespeare plays for him; he painted me songs. Outfitted only in his tee-shirt and socks on cold nights, I'd contribute a finger-roll and shimmy shake on tambourine, melding with his bluegrass banjo or pensive or peppery piano. I'd recite Lady Anne's soliloquy in a swooping *Swan Lake* dance, ending in a split on the ground where we'd have soulful, sweet sex that hurtled us galaxies beyond conscious grasp. Tucker cried out "long live John Keats!" at the height of our pleasure, which caused us to laugh so hard we fell fast asleep on the rug, waking by dawn when Socrates came to get a hug.

We'd sit outside on warm or cool still nights in the yard, alone or with friends, often with my head on his shoulder, jamming, breathing in the stars and sharing threads of our past that wove us into each other's present and offered a multihued future that might lead anywhere. His telescope was a gateway to see outer worlds; his eyes led me inward to depths unfathomable.

These years were hard for Rosemary. She was in a string of relationships, none of which really worked. First Scott, then Abebe, Aki, and then Rhonda. After she met someone, she would disappear from our lives only to reemerge months later in tears. When we were busy, she went to the community center.

"Angie, I'm going to be alone forever."

"Rosemary, you're an amazing person."

"Can't you just tell me I'm going to find someone?"

"But I don't know the future."

"God, you're so pragmatic!"

"I hope you'll find what you're looking for."

"You're so lucky that you have Tucker."

I was. I hugged her.

Geneviève bemoaned the unexplained loss of Johnny. The unknowing was a weight that caused her shoulders to slump. She and I struggled with guilt after Neil's suicide even though rationally we knew better. Our experience keyed us into the harrowing self-blame people feel after suicide.

Neil's son Sam was adrift. He robbed a house and did six months in juvenile hall. We searched for a male of his father's age to mentor for him. When young Robby learned of the situation, he stepped up and offered to coach Sam in track and field, which Sam had participated in when his dad was alive. Running proved transformational in Sam's life. Track gave him a community, confidence, and endorphins. It was beneficial for Robby too. I was so proud of him.

We kept up relationships with Kieran, and Tucker's parents in person, and mine remotely. I missed my folks, especially on birthdays and holidays, but they choose their life; I choose mine. Overall life was remarkable. Tucker and I were arguably the luckiest people on the planet.

II.

THE MESH MESS

The sun graced us with a warm and welcoming fall day. I spread my palms flat on the earth, pointed toes skyward, and eyed Tucker's trim abs as his tee-shirt draped down around his chest. I studied how his beautiful biceps shortened and flexed as he struggled to find a point of upside-down balance. He had no sooner kicked up into a handstand during morning yoga when his sinewy arms folded like the legs of a card table. He dropped on the grass, his hands over groin.

"Owwww."

Socrates bounded up and down, barking and whining, and licked Tucker's face.

"What's wrong? Is it your appendix?"

"What kind of crazy-ass anatomy classes have you taken? My appendix isn't in my testicles."

"Oh, no, what happened to your testicles?"

"Nothing. I think it might be a hernia."

Leaning on me like a crutch, Tucker hobbled to the car. We sped to his physician's office. He didn't say a word about my driving. As we waited for him to be fit into the schedule, he poked at the sore spot and grunted. An old woman with a drippy nose observed him as if he was going to be blinded for sinning. At the two-hour mark, the receptionist called, "Trucker Boy."

"Um. Yeah. Tucker Boyd." Drippy nose rolled her eyes, visibly relieved that we were leaving.

Dr. Brineman has a multitude of diplomas on his wall. When I squinted, they looked like my dad's post-it notes stuck *just so* in formation on the refrigerator door. I read a diploma on the top right. It was from junior high. The one next to it from high school. I'm surprised he didn't have a kindergarten report card up too. *Plays well with others.*

Or does he?

"Feel this?" Brineman grabbed my hand, pushed it onto a lump a smidge to the left of Tucker's crotch, and wiggled my fingers around. "This is an opening of muscle. The connective tissue needs to be surgically repaired. It's an inguinal hernia. Inner groin. Common in men. Some women too." Then, without offering to buy me a drink first, he placed his hand on my inguinal ligament and pressed firmly. "See? Yours is smooth." In what other field could a man touch a woman's crotch without asking?

Don't slap him, Angie. Focus on Tucker.

The doctor tossed off a few questions. Tucker guessed he got the hernia from carting around cameras and tripods. Brineman referred him to Dr. Ramon. "He's the surgical expert. *The* guy you need to go to. Call him stat," Brineman ordered. "If I ask, he'll fit you in as an emergency."

Tucker and I, in a haze of hurry, researched before making an appointment. I checked Dr. Ramon's profile on the Board of Registration in Medicine while Tucker buried himself in review sites. Ramon came up with a clean record from the board and, according to reviews, was adored. I drove Tucker to the consultation and sat in the waiting room catching up on store orders.

Tucker rejoined me and encapsulated the consultation. "He's got more diplomas and awards than Brineman."

Junior High diplomas? I wondered.

"He is pretty cocky about being an *expert* in hernia repair who has authored *dozens* of peer reviewed papers on the subject. Angie, I'm scared." He hadn't planned on surgery when he woke up happy and healthy that morning, I understood.

"Oh, here he is. Dr. Ramon, this is my wife, Angela."

The doctor, hair slicked and shiny with mineral oil, vigorously shook my hand. "It's not the worst I've seen, but not good. Not gonna get better on its own, right? Huh? Am I right? So, we operate at 7:00 a.m. tomorrow. Remember, no food, drink, or even a sip of water after midnight. NPO, right, huh?" He slapped Tucker on the back.

"Right." Tucker looked scared.

"Tomorrow? That's it? What do we need to know about this? Risks, choices?" I was incredulous.

"You're worrying too much, Angela. "I'm a surgical expert. It's a minimally invasive outpatient surgery. My technique is the gold standard. You're in good hands. Risks of not operating outweigh the normal risks of any surgery." Using his thumb and index finger, he formed what looked like a gun and pointed it at Tucker, "Poo. You're on track, buddy. Get some sleep. Wipe down with the antiseptic all over in the morning. Don't miss a spot. Okay? You got that, right?"

In the car, as I clicked my seatbelt on, I expressed doubts. "He's pushy, don't you think? And that hair."

"What am I supposed to do? It hurts. I can't stand upright. Brineman uses him all the time."

"I should've gone in with you. It's always good to have another set of ears."

"I was thorough. I shared my physical history like a PowerPoint presentation. I asked questions about risks and recovery."

I could imagine how Tucker's side of the conversation went. Ramon was arrogant though. When I mentioned that, Tuck said he wanted a confident surgeon and only trusted the one referred by his doctor. It was like he played defense against me.

I called Brineman's office and spoke with Jean, his office manager. "Jean, it's rushed. I'm worried."

"Angela, I understand your concern. If it was my Derek, I'd be protective too. This surgeon has an excellent reputation. He does state-of-the-art laparoscopic surgery. Tucker will be fine."

"I'd like to talk to Dr. Brineman."

"He's in with a patient."

"I'll wait as long as I need to."

Tucker curled into the car door, clutching his stomach. After five minutes, Brineman's voice came on. "Mrs. Boyd, no need to worry. Ramon is the best. The gold standard. It's a keyhole surgery. A few incisions, a few days of pain, and he'll be good as new. Get some rest tonight."

Right. Not much chance that will happen.

Tucker came out of anesthesia with a joke. "The gown doesn't go with my coloring. I'm a winter."

"You can tell a person's true nature by how they come out of surgery," Dr. Ramon's nurse said.

"Hi, Angela." Tucker white-knuckled my hand. His face was pale, but exactly an hour after he came to, Dr. Ramon sent us home as Tucker complained about sharp shooting pain in the area.

"You'll sleep, you'll feel better. Okay? Right? Mesh repair is easy." This seemed to be Ramon's whole schtick.

What, Nurse, can you tell about one's personality when they are in excruciating pain and pass out on the toilet after being sent home from an outpatient clinic? Is that due to the nature of the patient? Tucker crawled on his hands and knees to the bedroom, drenched in sweat. He was ice cold. "Oh, Tucker, lie down right here. I'll get a blanket and call 911."

"I don't want to go to the hospital," he cried.

"I'll stay right by your side. I'm with you, Tucker."

After blood and urine tests, a saline IV, and being hooked up to beeping heart monitors for eight hours in the ER, Tucker was discharged. I spoon-fed him broth for days. Looked after him like a mama lion just like with Simon, my Seal Point Siamese kitten. Got people to help at the store.

While Tucker tried to sleep (unsuccessfully due to pain), I read about laparoscopic hernia surgery. "They cover the hernia with mesh from within the abdomen and staples are commonly fired through it into the muscle tissue in order to fix it as a patch." Dr. Ramon never told any of this to us while he rushed Tucker in as though his gut would burst if we waited a day.

Tucker writhed in pain. I tried to get answers from medical providers. We were told, "Dr. Ramon is the best. He says the operation was successful," then asked, "Has Tucker ever had anxiety?"

Anxiety? Tucker? No. It was at this point, I smelled a rat.

Tucker, always health-conscious, attempted to eat his usual healthy diet. He was the chef, and I, chief bottlewasher and salad maker, so when he couldn't eat due to pain and nausea, I taught myself to make him his own soups. I contributed two recipes from Lena: lentil - vegetable soup and squash - garbanzo bean soup, the one that birthed the name of my bookstore. As the weeks went on, his pain levels remained high. He couldn't work or function normally.

"My life is over. That guy destroyed me."

"I'll find you help. There has to be a way to fix this. Hang in there. I love you."

I worked round the clock to adjust to take care of both of us, fill out paperwork, talk to doctors. Unexpected medical bills arrived like roaches. Ramon tripled the price of surgery. I called the insurance, but they didn't care. The sight of Ted, our mail carrier, now made me nauseous. *Bills. Bills. Bills.* I needed answers. Something was wrong, but no one would admit to anything.

I hired Veronika, a bubbly woman with a smile that heals as well as her hands, to give Tucker a weekly massage at the house. The bodywork momentarily helped to alleviate tension in the rest of his body, but not in his gut. He breathed, visualized, and chanted, but didn't improve. This medical device had cruel effects on my husband.

"What did I do to deserve this?" Tucker inquired repeatedly.

Whenever he asked this question, my chest constricted like I'd been pierced with a poisoned dart. I held his face in my hands and kissed his head. "Nothing, Tucker. Nothing. The bad things that happen to people on this earth do not correlate to their actions. You trusted a doctor you were referred to. You trusted that having his medical board's license in good standing was an indication of an ethical professional. We didn't know at that time how the system works."

"Angela, why won't anyone admit to or believe I'm in agonizing pain? The denial fuzzes up my head. It's making me crazy."

Over the next several years, we connected with people like us who were harmed by medical devices or other medical malpractice. They educated us about this systemwide corruption. People who bring valid civil lawsuits are gagged, threatened, slandered, and sued by the offending doctor for defamation. Medical boards, their experts, defense and even some plaintiff lawyers, judges, FDA, FDIC, police, D.A.s, insurance companies, and legislators collude or stand by.

Kay Dean's *Fake Review Watch* on YouTube educated us on how doctors employ reputation management to get bad reviews down and fake good ones up. When Tucker looked up Dr. Ramon, he had no way of knowing that reviews were paid and faked. There are doctors who care and save or improve lives, but the system is antiquated, ignores prevention, and treats victims and survivors worse than criminals. A strong group of individuals in California call their medical board regularly and work tirelessly to ensure that other consumers will not meet their sad fate.

We met parents whose daughters were killed in childbirth by repeat offenders. Sepsis is often ignored. We learned that a hair-growing formula can cause lifelong impotence. Fat removal, used in many medically recommended operations, causes an increase in disease-producing tissue. People die or become ill from gadolinium. Carcinogens such as nickel, beryllium, chromium, and mercury are still used in some dental practices. We met a woman in Australia who was told she needed a hysterectomy for cancer, but she didn't have cancer. This apparently is common. Removing body parts for any reason causes a negative change in hormones that affects health. Breast implants wreak havoc for many women. The list of harmful procedures is extensive.

Tucker got involved in the movement. Weak and in agony, from his bed, he made calls.

I struggled to keep up a semblance of normal life. I wanted to take care of Tucker full time, but I had my business to run. I managed less time at the store, and more days dedicated to him. Our savings and retirement plan were being drained. I kept up with the talk line remotely because the political-social climate was on high alert, Geneviève needed me, and it was a chance to get out of my own family's devastation as a respite. One day, the role of listen-ee and listener reversed.

"Hello, North Yarmouth Grief and Support Line. This is Angela. What's your name?"

"Osheena."

"Hi, Osheena. That's such a pretty name. What's going on for you tonight?"

"The holidays are a bad time for me. I lost my parents five years ago in an accident. All my friends have new marriages and babies."

"So, they don't include you anymore?"

"No. They invite me over, but I don't want to go sit around with crying babies and grouchy husbands. I want to go out and party."

"That sucks not to have anyone to go out with. Do you mind me asking how old you are?"

"Twenty-three."

"All your friends are already married at twenty-three?"

"Yeah, can you believe it? Those fools. How old are you? Are you married?"

"Thirty-four. Yes, I am."

"You have kids?" A minute went by. "Hello? You still there? You have kids?"

"N... n... no. Just worried about my husband."

"Oh, no! I'm sorry. Here I call and make the talk line operator cry!"

"It's okay. Life happens, Osheena. Everyone's got something to deal with."

"Shoot. My problems are nothing."

"There is no comparison one person to the next. Your feelings are valid. I apologize. I'm just tired. I'm here Tuesday and Wednesday nights from 6:00 to midnight. Call me anytime."

"You're only human, right. I'll call you again sometime and we can chat. I like you. Take care of yourself."

"You, too. Goodnight."

Click.

Tucker found a well-done study which concluded that eleven percent of patients who have mesh-based inguinal hernia surgery experience chronic pain. Hernia mesh can cause adhesions, bowel obstruction or perforation, rejection, migration, and be life-threatening. Laparoscopic or open repair can be performed with or without surgical mesh, but Dr. Ramon rushed Tucker in like the forest was on fire. He minimized and denied our concerns. And lied.

Over the next two weeks we went to three pricy specialists. Each one covered for the surgeon. The months swooshed past like cars on the Autobahn and still *no answers.* Tucker lived in pain and terror. "I awoke to a nightmare and I'm a burden to you."

"You are a treasure to me. I want to find a way to help you."

My call shifts kept me grounded. It was a gift to be there for others as we struggled along too. When Geneviève called to wish us a Happy New Year, I let loose like a band of wild monkeys. "We're going out of our minds! These people are crazy! No one does anything! What the hell is happening?" When I caught my breath, she spoke her first words since "Happy New Year."

"Have you seen *Gaslight* with Ingrid Bergman, Charles Boyer, and Joseph Cotton?"

"Yes. Bergman is an absolute revelation, no news there. She nailed this role. My favorite scene is when she desperately rummages in her handbag and the pin isn't there. Why do you ask?"

"This is what they're doing to you and Tucker."

"What?"

"Gaslighting."

"Gaslighting!"

"Making you think that you're crazy. DARVO. Denying and reversing victim and offender. Making you question your reality. Portraying a slanderous version of you both. The current-day medical field is notorious for this. They will act do anything to CYA."

"CYA?"

"Means "cover your ass." They cover their ass. Protect their own. They'll say risks were presented. Medicine is an art, not a science. The procedure was perfect. You're overly protective and have Munchausen syndrome. Tucker has mental problems. Factitious disorder. He's physically fine, but he's a worrier. Maybe he was sick before. Maybe he does this for attention."

"But he's not okay. He wasn't sick! He's not a worrier. You know him! He's..."

"Oh course, I know. You see how they got you on the defensive already? You're preaching to the choir here. I know your husband, *the mayor*!"

"Yes, the mayor!"

"What does the consent form say?"

"I don't know. Not what they did. Brineman confirmed Ramon uses mesh. We never heard of mesh. Ramon never *once* mentioned it. How could we research or consent if we didn't know?"

"Can I come over?"

"Yes. Please. Whenever you can. You mean *now*? Aren't you going out for New Years?"

"Angela, the world is in crisis. The phones are ringing off the hook. My right-hand gal is dealing with catastrophe. I'll ring in the new year monitoring the new volunteers you trained, and then I'm coming over there to see what the hell is going on. I'm so sorry about all of this."

Tucker watched "The Chocolate Factory" episode of *I Love Lucy* while Geneviève and I poured through the medical papers. He always laughed when Lucy shoves the extra candy in her mouth. He didn't laugh. He couldn't even do a crossword puzzle.

Geneviève was apoplectic. "You have to get his full records. Find a doctor who'll do the right exams." She scoured the Internet for possible doctors who might be honest, but with New Year's upon us, we were in a holding pattern.

I tucked Tucker in bed and geared up for my talk line shift. Geneviève stayed to clean up and keep me company while I answered calls. She smelled the fear in me.

"Hello, North Yarmouth Grief and Support Talk Line. This is Angela. What's your name?"

"Uh... it's Bill from Giovanni's. Your order is ready: three large pizzas, one cheese, one full vegetable, no mushrooms, one sausage, pepperoni and green pepper. Two Caesar salads, large, two antipastos. Total $87.43. For pick up or delivery?"

"Delivery. The North Yarmouth Community Support Center. Treating the workers tonight. Full house."

"On Bridgeport?"

"Yes. You can pull around the back."

"We'll be there in twenty minutes. No charge."

"No charge?"

"Your team is working a grief and support talk line on New Year's? No charge. It's on us. Happy New Year."

"Thank you. Same to you, Bill."

Click.

"Hello, North Yarmouth Grief and Support Talk Line. This is Angela. What's your name?"

"Lou. You want to hear my New Year's resolution?"

"Sure."

"I resolved to kill myself this year."

"I'm sorry to hear that, Lou. What's going on?"

"Wife died, daughter is teaching in Africa. She's a do-gooder. Barely get to see her. Don't feel so good. Retired, bored. Shall I go on?"

"Is that Poco in the background?"

"Yeah."

"I love Poco."

"Me too."

"I haven't heard them in so long."

"I got everything by them."

"Do you have "Picking Up the Pieces"?"

"Yeah."

"Would you play it for me? It's a wonderful song."

"Sure. Hang on."

I heard shuffling noises, then the music came on. We both sang along.

"Richie Furay. Love that guy."

"Do you play music, Lou?"

"Yep. Juice harp, banjo. Country."

"Do you have friends to play with?"

"No. They're all gone. Well, maybe Marty.... hmm.... maybe I'll give Marty a call."

"Lou, where did your daughter learn to be a do-gooder?"

"From me and my wife. Hmm. There's a kids' hospital and a group home near me. I thought of... hmm... I thought of seeing if they'd like to hear some music."

"If you're in crisis, call a crisis line. Otherwise, take care of yourself and let me know how the music goes at the kids' hospital, okay?"

"Hmm. Yep. Sure will. What was your name again?"

"Angela. I'm here on Tuesdays and Wednesdays from 6:00 p.m. to midnight. Call me anytime."

"Happy New Year, Angela."

"Happy New Year, Lou."

Click.

Tucker canceled his last follow-up appointment with Dr. Ramon. He packed the smallest of a set of navy suitcases we had bought for traveling the world to study culture, language, and search for rare or beautiful birds. "Take me to the emergency room in Boston," he insisted.

The waiting room was crowded and noisy. All the seats were filled. It was like an airport without the fun trip. Tucker and I checked in with reception every half hour, reminding them of his physical agony and inability to continue to stand in his condition.

"Sorry, sir, you are not priority."

After a hellish four hours of waiting, Tucker walked over to reception, asked for help, and was *again* denied it. He doubled over and screamed, "I NEED HELP! I can't stand it. The – pain - is - unbearable. I'm weak, dizzy, and on the verge of fainting."

An aide parked him on a gurney in the hall under fluorescent lights. I insisted on going with him.

"The rooms are all filled. Wait here," she said.

Moans came from all directions. It was like being an extra in a horror movie. Tucker was hungry and exhausted. A nurse walked him through someone's room to a bathroom. He came out wearing a paper gown and holding his urine in a cup. The nurse took the cup and his clothes, shoes, pumpkin seeds, and water away.

"What are you doing with my clothes? It's freezing in here."

"We took them so you won't hurt yourself."

"Hurt himself?"

"Hurt myself?"

"You're set up with a psych consult. Do you have a history of panic?"

"No. I called yesterday and explained my situation. Isn't there a record of this?"

"A doctor will be with you soon."

"What kind of fucking answer is that?"

An hour later, Ha, a deer-in-the-headlights psych resident and her psychiatrist consultant showed up. Naïve and optimistic, Tucker was eager to share his story. Ha redirected him, so she didn't get an accurate history. He was distraught. She treated his upset as a psychiatric problem.

Ha pulled me aside. "He's calm and cooperative, but his mood is anxious. His affect is full with inappropriate smiling and his thought process is circumstantial and overly inclusive."

"Your contradictory speculations are all over the place. You kept interrupting him! Why don't you listen? He was healthy before the surgical harm." Rage erupted through me like volcanic lava.

Ha scurried away, writing bullshit notes that would go in Tucker's medical record. A woman with a grey pallor, in a chaplain's uniform, approached Tucker. "What is your religious background?"

"Why, are you here to perform last rites?"

"No, sir. I'm here to provide support through prayer."

"I'm non-denominational. I came in for an exam, not prayer."

"My prayers are non-denominational," the chaplain said with a patronizing calm.

"He doesn't want prayer." She glared at me like I was a sinner.

"I'm here to get an exam due to pain from hernia mesh that was used without my knowledge."

Dr. Terry, the ER doctor arrived. "What's going on here?"

Tucker told him all the problems caused by the mesh. His chief complaint was physical pain, but the doctor refused to do an AXIS III assessment. He concluded code 300.00: anxiety. Tucker grabbed my arm like he was hanging from a cliff. He had a wild, terrified look in his eyes, "It's a cuckoo's nest. Get me out of here."

"I want to leave," Tucker told an aide. "I'll never get help here." Before she discharged him, a nurse asked what his pain level was on a scale of 0 – 10. She didn't give him a context with which to base his answer. "Far beyond a ten," he said.

"I'll write nine," she said.

"Fine, whatever," he said, as he swallowed anxiety medication he didn't want or need in order to leave.

End note in chart: *Patient discharged home accompanied by sister. Pain 0 on a scale of 0-10. Discharge teaching completed.* All wrong.

The next week he went to see Dr. Helena Cortez for a common sleep medication. Since Dr. Brineman wouldn't acknowledge the surgical harm, Tucker had to see a psychiatrist to get the medication. Her office was in a drab, boxy building with bad parking. Forgettable abstract art hung in her waiting room. Tucker pushed a buzzer and announced himself. After a few minutes, a woman battling unseen demons rushed out.

Dr. Cortez called Tucker in. She had a tight ponytail and thick glasses. She gestured for us to sit in overstuffed chairs by windows that flaunt an impressive view. A bird flew by, free. Tucker eyed it with envy. He explained to Dr. Cortez about the problems from the mesh. Helena Cortez blinked a lot. I wondered if she had dry eyes or stress? She flipped her ponytail back to front.

"Tell me about all the trauma in your life."

"Trauma?"

"Yes, your history."

"I'm not here for psychotherapy or psych drugs. I need sleep medication due to the pain."

"I need to know your history. Tell me everything."

"Why? Before the mesh," he said, "I was healthy, high-functioning, and productive. No anxiety or mood problems or anything else."

At $250 cash per hour, Helena Cortez put Tucker on eleven unneeded, overlapping medications in used, dirty bottles within three months. She left him barely able to function, think, or move. Each time the medication wore off, it caused jitters. He told Cortez. She said it was all anxiety.

"Tucker, why do you even take these awful pills?"

"I'm desperate, Angie. I hope something will lessen the pain." *He was addled by the meds.*

Tucker fell several times due to the harm to his body and bad polypharma effects. Dr. Cortez misdiagnosed him as an agoraphobe.

"You should take walks alone, without your wife, to rebuild neural pathways. What's the worst that can happen? You'll pass out and hit your head? So what? Someone will find you eventually and call the paramedics."

"Tucker is an extrovert. We call him the mayor of New York. If you want to help," I said to Dr. Cortez, "insist that his doctor orders MRIs."

There was that volcanic rage again. I had heartburn. Dr. Cortez flipped her hair, leaned into Tucker and said, "I'm going to give you medication until I FIX you." She held up two bottles to Tucker and asked him, "Which is better, *this* or *this*?"

Tucker had reached his limit. His nostrils flared like the horse he'd photographed in Delaware. "The pills made me vomit, have gripping stomachaches, body zaps, headaches, ringing ears, see and hear double, feel crazy and feel terrible in all aspects. Neither is better. Stop poisoning me. I've thrown up so much from these meds you're plying me with, I'm wasting away. Are you *trying* to kill me? I can no longer tolerate light. I wear sunglasses in a dark house."

Dr. Cortez leaned in again and squinted at his eyes, "Your pupils look pretty that way."

A week after Tucker told her to stop poisoning him, she closed her practice. She reopened it in three months. What Tucker needed was a new primary care doctor, but we had trouble finding someone with integrity. People in online medical harm groups said that patients are often blacklisted after they report medical malpractice. Psychiatrists took on the victims though. They labeled healthy people as crazy and made a lot of money from it. *What a racket.*

"Hello, North Yarmouth Grief and Support Line. This is Angela. What's your name?"

"Suzette."

"Hi, Suzette. What's going on tonight?"

"Angela, I'm *deeply* sad. We're in a dark place as a human race. I'm afraid to see how nature and people will be ruined. The poor get tossed onto the street while the elite drink champagne."

"Did something happen recently that made you feel this way?"

"Yes. A friend of mine is homeless now. She worked hard all her life and then a doctor hurt her. It's ruined her life."

I thought of Ramon, Brineman, Ha, and Cortez.

"Suzette, I'm so sorry. I get a lot of calls about harm from doctors. I'm experiencing this in my own family. It's unconscionable that the government lets this go on. What is your friend's name?"

"Emily. Always the brightest light in the room. She's so desperate she wants to kill herself. I want her live with us, but we don't have room. Three kids, two-bedroom house, but how can you say no when a friend is on the street? What if it were me? What if it was you, Angela?"

"I don't know. Something. What are you going to do?"

"I told my husband we need to get a trailer. Park it in front of the house. Give her a roof anyway. Little bit of safety, dignity."

"That sounds doable. Do you take care of yourself, Suzette?"

"I do. I eat well, exercise, have my family and knitting group."

"I'm here Tuesday and Wednesday nights from 6:00 to midnight. If you feel like it, call me sometime and let me know how you and Emily are."

"That's sweet of you. I'll call back. Give you an update. Bye."

Click.

"Hello, North Yarmouth Grief and Support Line. This is Angela. What's your name?"

"Hey, babe. It's me."

"Hi Tucker. Is everything okay?"

"No. I'm dizzy and nauseous."

"Stay seated or lying down. Do you need to call 911?"

"No."

"I'm coming right home. Love you."

"Love you more."

Click.

12.

HEY, SHAMAN!

Just after 2:00 p.m. there was a lull in the store. I scurried home to give Tucker some veggie soup. The day began badly with his laments that he had been a bad person in a past life and was now being punished for it. I phoned to let him know I was coming. There was no answer.

As I pulled up in front, I heard primal banging and wailing emanating from our house. It wasn't anything from Tucker's vast collection of music or any of his instruments or voice, but rather it was intense growling, howling, and pounding of a drum. I flung open the door to see Tucker laid out on our couch cushions that were lined up horizontally on the floor. His thinness was camouflaged by a thick cotton hooded sweatshirt, wool socks, and a wool beanie. He thrashed like a sick baby seal and grabbed at his side as he did when the pain was elevated.

"Oh my god, Tucker. Are you all right! What's happened? Why are you on the floor?"

"*Shhhh*, you're disrupting the energy. We're quieting his mind so he can hear the magic of the life force." My attention turned to a man about thirty-five who was sitting cross-legged on the floor. He wore white flowy pants, a white tunic, beaded necklaces and bracelets, a feather behind the ear, and a claw of some kind around his neck. He PA-POOMed on his drum for emphasis.

"Who are you? What the hell is going on here?"

Tucker lifted his head. He looked unrecognizable to the man I had married. "I called Shaman Jeff. Marfusa kept telling me that I needed a shaman. She says my soul is scattered."

"Marfusa?! That crazy, imbalanced, superstitious woman you met online in a patient harm group? *She* told you to call someone to bang on a drum and howl like a wolf in our living room?"

"Hey, I'm a trained shaman. I'm helping your husband. I've been gathering pieces of his soul that are scattered throughout time and space. As traumas occur, we lose pieces of ourselves. This causes spiritual illness. He cannot heal until the pieces of his soul are retrieved."

"Uh-huh. Uh-huh. Trained where? At a workshop on Coney Island?"

"Yes, actually. It was a transformative workshop."

"And you're charging how much for this hoodwinking?"

"It's five hundred dollars for the spiritual services, mam."

"Five... get out." I pointed to the door. "You're taking financial and emotional advantage of my husband who is medically injured, scared and hurting."

I squatted to help Tucker up. "My god, you're shaking, sweating, and parched. Did you have water today? Have you eaten? Let's get you into bed. Jeff. Hey, shaman! Hook your arm under his other arm and help me get him up."

Jeff, who apparently had the secrets of the universe at his beck and call and stunk of myrrh, hadn't had the common sense to refrain from putting my weak and confused husband on sofa cushions.

"Just please hook your arm under his and help me lift. If anything happens to him from this, I will hold you liable."

Shaman Jeff clicked his mouth to indicate the degree to which my lack of shamanic spirituality awareness sucked. The defiant jut of his chin communicated that I was the reason that Tucker was in this mess. Poor un-woke me.

"One, two, three," I counted.

I got Tucker safely to his bed and gave him half a glass of water because his lips cracked when he was dehydrated. "Drink this. I'll be right back."

In the living room, Jeff was still standing in his socked feet with a white scarf dramatically woven around his neck.

"I take cash, check, or credit card."

My voice dropped to a vicious whisper. "Real healers don't charge money for rituals and sure as hell don't take advantage of a vulnerable person. Disturbing our neighborhood and filling my husband whose body was seriously injured full of fear about *fractured* pieces of his soul is *not* a loving thing to do. Now GET - THE - FUCK - OUT - OF - MY - HOUSE."

This passive-aggressive greedy fake purposefully moved slowly to irritate me. He gathered up his hand drums, maracas, singing bowl, and leaf rattle and faced me defiantly. This was not a principled man. Tucker would've spotted this schemer miles away before his life was altered.

"What are you waiting for? Leave!" I again pointed my finger like a laser to the door. "Oh, on second thought, do you have a card?"

"Yes." He handed me a card with a symbol of a hand on it that looked like a hieroglyphic.

"You can mail the payment here. Five hundred dollars." He put his finger on his address.

"If we so much as see or hear from you again, Jeff, I will take out a restraining order and sue you. My husband is terrified and you have done nothing but harm him. You should be ashamed."

After I shut the door behind Jeff Zincky with a P.O. Box on Long Island, he took out a smudge stick, lit it, and hostilely flicked some sage puffs towards the door. Then, he moved the sage around his head and up and down his arms and legs. When he got to his chest, the embers caught some material. The last I saw of Jeff the charlatan shaman he was patting his singed gauze scarf.

I rushed back to Tucker. "I'm sorry. I know you're terrified. We'll figure something out. Magical thinking isn't the answer. There has a to be a decent doctor who will prescribe sleep medication without using you as a chemical lab. Tomorrow I'm meeting with Geneviève and her social psychologist friend. He's coming to town just for you. Do you want us to bring him by the house after we meet?"

"Yes. Tell him I already cut down on that poison medication. Now I think I'm in withdrawal. There was nothing wrong with me. Just the mesh and medical harm."

"I know, Tucker. I know."

"Hi James," I greeted our waiter at Picky Eaters as Geneviève as I crumbled fresh chamomile and mint in hot water. My shoulders dropped about two inches as I sipped the tea. "Dr. Cardellini, it's out of control. These doctors have been throwing chemicals at Tucker's brain. It's completely insane and abusive. He's not depressed. He's hurt. By doctors. By *them!*"

"Call me Antonio. This is terrible. It's become the norm for the psychiatric community to treat healthy people with physical injuries as though they are mentally disturbed and to wrongly prescribe and overprescribe to the most vulnerable people. They're creating casualties."

"Who cares if you go to school for ten years if you come out full of assumptions and bias?" Geneviève poured honey in her tea as if to drown out the bitterness of Tucker's situation.

I was relieved to have Antonio, a respected expert in his field, take the time to meet with us. His jaw was long and he had a thin scar on his chin that added to his seriousness. "Psychiatric drugs can be helpful for some people in some situations, preferably in acute crisis and short-term, but in a fundamentally different way than what we're told about various biological abnormalities. They occupy receptors, but it's not possible to selectively target one receptor and even if it was, it wouldn't be helpful to Tucker's body. No biological magic is happening."

"Right, it's biological abuse!"

Antonio exuded a gentle strength. "Psychiatry began as a form of social control; heartless, judgmental, racist, classist, and concerned about money and power. The Joint Commission on Mental Illness and Mental Health once said, 'this is a field where fads and fancies flourish.'

"In 1951, Senator Humphrey cosponsored an amendment to the FDA that significantly expanded the list of medications that can only be obtained with a doctor's prescription. This turned doctors into drug vendors with a much more privileged status in society. Drug companies began showering them and their doctors' organizations with marketing dollars. The American Medical Association dropped its critical stance toward the industry immediately. They didn't even require drugmakers to prove drugs were effective."

"No wonder we're in such a mess in this country." Geneviève's lip scowled like Elvis singing "Don't Be Cruel."

Antonio continued, "Ads in journals exaggerated benefits and obscured risks. Pharmaceutical companies ghostwrote the articles. The purposes of psych drugs were to make hospitalized patients easier to handle, to turn them into complicit zombies."

"The doctors are trying to control Tucker's emotions and reduce the intensity and they've nearly killed him. They don't listen to him. He's in intractable pain."

"One problem your husband faces is that the body adapts to the drugs; withdrawal can be harrowing. The solution is gradual tapering. His attention will be pulled to the pain. He'll have to learn to coexist with it. He needs to take care of his health and focus on things he loves doing."

I was hit by a wave of queasiness and couldn't eat my breakfast. "He blames himself. Thinks he did something bad in a past life, because he sure as hell didn't do anything bad in this one."

Antonio was perceptive. "You're both entitled to be angry, sad, or numb. All emotions are okay. Neither of you created this. I can share my knowledge and you decide what to do. Let's wrap our food and go. I'd like to meet your husband as soon as possible. I'm here to support him."

On the way to the car, Anthony asked, "Out of curiosity, have you heard of Dr. David Rosenhan?"

"Yes, in school. He did the experiment in 1973 where he and some other people checked themselves into a mental hospital?"

"Rosenhan and seven other 'normal' people went to mental hospitals. They behaved calmly but feigned auditory hallucinations in the interview process only. They all were admitted to a psychiatric hospital. Once there, they behaved normally. All but one pseudo-patient was diagnosed as schizophrenic. Rosenhan said, 'We now know that we cannot diagnose sanity from insanity.'"

Noticing the chess set, Antonio challenged Tucker to a game. This was a smart way to bond because Tucker didn't trust anyone anymore. They played in semi-darkness because of Tucker's light insensitivity. Antonio rehashed our conversation from earlier. Tucker moved his bishop.

"I'm in a hell of a situation. I'm going to have to exist in my mind because I can't live in these hell levels of pain I'm in. I didn't know that people could even survive in this much pain."

"Unfortunately, I don't have a solution for you on that, but I'm hopeful we'll be able to reduce your suffering caused by wrongly prescribed medication. I gave Angela my number. Call me without hesitation. Also, I spoke to Dr. Hollifield. He'll meet with you this week. He's a good man. It's a bit of a drive, but after the initial exam, you'll be able to do teleconferences."

"Thank you, Antonio. I've been on a rollercoaster for months. Checkmate."

"What?"

"I just cornered your king."

"Ah, so you did. And this is you under duress? You're remarkable, Tucker."

Indeed.

I hugged Geneviève goodbye. "This is the first time I can breathe in months. I'm wrung out, though."

"Take care of yourself. I'm a call away."

An hour after Geneviève and Antonio left, I crawled into bed in the office. Tucker looked for me. He was encouraged for the first time in ages.

"Angela? Are you okay?" I didn't respond. I motioned to the thermometer on the desk. "102!" He felt my forehead. His hand felt good, like the cool wash of a mountain creek. "You're burning up. Do you need to go to the doctor?"

No. I shook my head. I was too tired to stand.

"What should I do?" He wrung his hands like a child. I didn't have the energy to speak. As damaged as he was, he would have to figure it out. He brought me a bedside pitcher, covered me with my favorite quilt, a basin in case I threw up, and held a cool washcloth on my forehead. He heated up pea soup, but it'd be days before I could eat. While gripping his side, shaking from withdrawal, and hobbling, my husband cared for me.

We were both glad to see night fall. "Here is a tambourine. Shake it if you need me. It will wake me up." A tambourine. Tucker's solution for everything was music.

I had a vivid dream of flying over the Andes. I awoke at 3:00 a.m. to go to the bathroom. The room whirled if I moved an inch. I didn't want to call Tucker. *Just move slowly, Angela. Don't call Tucker. Let him sleep. Don't call him. Don't think of pink elephants. Don't call Tucker.* "Tuck-hurrrrrrr!!! Hurry!!" I shook the tambourine like a salsa dancer in a fire. *Shhh-shhhh-shhhhh-sha-sha. Shhh-shhhh-shhhhh-sha-sha.*

Tucker ran in with maracas. *Cha-cha-cha. Cha-cha-cha.* I was burning up to high heaven, but my husband made me laugh. *Shhh-*

shhhh-shhhhh-sha-sha. Shhh-shhhh-shhhhh-sha-sha. Cha-cha-cha. Cha-cha-cha. Shhh-shhhh-shhhhh-sha-sha. Shhh-shhhh-shhhhh-sha-sha. Cha-cha-cha. Cha-cha-cha. "I love you. I am the luckiest and unluckiest person in the world."

"Perhaps."

Nine months after the operation, we met Dr. Hollifield, a short, energetic, curly-haired fellow. A direct man. He did several exams and tests and said, "He mangled your insides. The mesh is migrating, causing bleeding and increased perforation of your intestine. For a lawsuit, you need repair surgery, but in your case, it's not feasible and would make things worse. Here, you can see the damage on the scans. Feel free to get several other opinions if you want."

"A lawsuit or surgery?" Tucker was shattered by these words. "These are my choices?"

"I'm concerned about mesh rejection and mesh shrinkage. Rejection may make you very ill."

"Mesh shrinkage? We didn't even know he was going to use mesh!" I paced like an angry tiger caged up for a Las Vegas review.

"I want this horrible mesh out of me!" Now Tucker was on his feet too. *"Get it out!"*

Hollifield's hand was warm and comforting on my arm. He addressed Tucker. "Your reactions are normal and healthy. I will be your treating doctor and prescribe the sleeping medication you need. Keep you away from doctors who throw medications at you that you don't need."

When I was with Jack, I forgot to remove my diaphragm after sex. My fingers are shorter than my cervix and I couldn't reach it. I begged Jack to meet me on a break from his production to fish it out. It was humiliating, disempowering, and caused me panic, which is not my normal state of mind. I could not imagine how Tucker felt with this sinister device inside him. *Forever.*

Dr. Hollifield's voice snapped me back to the present. "I'll need to meet with you every three months to renew your medication. I wish you could sue that HODAD for millions of dollars, but medical malpractice lawsuits are very hard to win."

"HODAD?"

"Hands Of Death And Destruction. That's what we call doctors like the POS who did this to Tucker. Look it up. And while you're at it look up medical malpractice, the third leading cause of death. Although it's more than that. They don't even count ambulatory centers or all of the injuries and deaths that are covered up."

"I will," I said.

"I just want my life back," Tucker said.

"I know. I'm sorry," Dr. Hollifield, a doctor with compassion and integrity, said.

I moved like a dancer, grabbed a napkin and plate for Tucker in first arabesque, pirouetted to return to the kitchen for knife and spoon, then out of ballerina mode and into Bollywood, boom, with a thumka, sideways pelvic thrust, I jutted my hip to shut the silverware drawer. I wore my runners all the time by then. There was little time to think, reflect, or mourn. The thoughts I did have were of my husband, the mayor. All I wanted was to sit and be with him. Hold his hand. Talk about birds, the weather, the morning's crossword puzzle, anything. I savored him. Looked past his gaunt cheeks into his endless soulful eyes. He was my world. I was his, but I was slowly being shut out. Pain, a wicked thief, was his mistress. I stared at the portrait of Sheba for solidarity and strength. We belong to a privileged club of women who enjoyed time with Tucker. Maybe he was so good our time was rationed. No one got a long lifetime of Boyd bliss.

One evening when the bookshop was empty, I closed it and drove home twenty minutes early. I wanted to surprise Tucker. I pulled up in front of the house and sat in the car updating my day planner before going inside. I'd learned that the moment I walked in, the dance began anew, so anything extra was relegated to time outside. My little electric automobile was my office. My run in the woods, my therapy. The bookstore and the community center, my social time. Our home was nearly single-pointedly a place to care for Tucker. Any disappointments or worries were dropped at the door because Tuck absorbed any upset I had, so I was a beacon for him. At first, I faked smiles when I wanted to cry. I consoled in favor of being consoled.

In time, my smile returned. The process of getting there was long, uneven, and took a backward turn at a moment's notice. My survival plan was to be present. *For better or for worse.*

Tucker's formerly sculpted forearms were now scrawny like chicken bones; his muscles wasted away. When he played guitar though, his weakened body transformed into a joyful vessel as the music uplifted our spirits. His singing, profound yet simple, resonated with the likes of Robert Johnson, Sonny Boy Williamson, Aaron Carter, and Woody Guthrie, musicians he so revered.

It was a new moon. The house was silhouetted against a bank of black velvet. Tucker and Socrates were in the kitchen. Tucker arranged the vegetables for me to chop.

He petted Socrates, gave him a treat. Removed the wilting flowers from the vase on the table and arranged those remaining in a fan. I knew he did this for me. In his way, he always had me in mind too.

Then he pirouetted and down he went! *Oh my gosh, he fell!* I clicked open the car door, grabbed my bag and keys, and bolted for the door. Before I got there, I heard Socrates' bark and whine. But then, Tucker was back up. He recovered himself. Gave Socrates another treat. "Good boy," I was close enough to see the words form on his lips. I stood back in the shadows like a voyeur, watching my husband as he navigated his loss of bodily control. "Worse every day like a lobster being boiled in a pot," he had explained. I took four deep breaths, and gently opened the door.

"How was your day, my love?" His limp was a bit more pronounced as he greeted me with the boyish abandon of any loving husband delighted to see his wife.

"Hectic, interesting, and dull at the end. I counted the minutes until I could come home and we could be together. How are you doing? Is there anything I can do for you?"

"Just take care of yourself," Tucker said. "The vegetables are ready. I'll just go lie down while you and Socrates go for a walk." And that was it. He never mentioned his fall. I wonder what else he never mentioned to me that he struggled with? I didn't ask because I wanted him to have the dignity to greet me like a king welcoming his queen. I didn't ask because I loved him.

Socrates and I enjoyed long talks though. As soon as I clicked on his leash, he began barking, telling me of his day. Dogs need someone to talk to, too.

The phases of Tucker's pain, disability, and medical mistreatment swelled and crashed in on us. Rosemary was an outstanding support to us emotionally and in terms of casseroles, which are crucial during trying times. All that was required from me was to scoop two portions with a slotted spoon, heat for three minutes, and ladle food into Rose Medallion bowls, and there we had it. Food to keep our bodies going while we pushed through the drawn-out days as we longed for those six or seven sweet hours of reprieve in the cradling, calming, delicious dark of night.

Tucker found that due to the pain, even a shred of light kept him from falling asleep or awakened him. Before the operation, he used to fall asleep anywhere, anytime - on a plane, on a train, standing up, cross-legged on a picnic in bright sunlight, and once, unfortunately while attending a living story at Bean There. Granted, the speaker spoke like a slowpoke and revealed the crux of her story – her aunt was in fact her biological mother and her assumed mother was her grandmother - after forty minutes. I had to elbow him awake.

In reading about sleep patterns, we learned that sensory deprivation, in which one is shielded from external stimuli such as sight and sound, helps. Due to the fluorescent streetlight on the streetcorner catty-corner to our cottage, beams of light slipped through the slats of the shutters into our bedroom, the room where Tucker slept. I'd been sleeping in the guest room/office with the crystals instead of with my husband because noise, touch, or movement disturbed his sleep.

Transitioning me out of our bedroom happened in stages. First, I rolled a cot into our room so I could remain close to him. At the slightest movement from me, Tucker bolted upright in bed and was unable to go back to sleep until he took another dose of medicine. We were together in the house round the clock, yet I missed our cozy and physical connection from before the mesh.

It came down to either replacing the shutters with blackout curtains that would mar the glow of vitamin D-rich heartening daylight or blocking out every bit of space on the windows during nocturnal hours. We chose the latter. We devised an ingenious formula for shutting out every bead of brightness during hours of slumber.

"Barry's Box City has 55x65-inch pieces of cardboard. We can cut pieces to fit into each of the windows," Tucker suggested. His mind was always working, desperate for a solution to his sleep woes.

"What do we do with the cardboard pieces during the day?"

"Lean them up against the wall."

"That will be an eyesore."

"Yes, but I'll be rested. A few more nights without decent sleep and I'm going to start hallucinating and seeing you as a common Blue Meanie in jackboots and spurs."

"'Yellow Submarine' reference?"

"Yes."

"Hello, Barry? Do you deliver your sheets of cardboard? Great. I'd like four pieces of the biggest ones you have."

The cardboards helped, but the light shone in from the top and sides.

"What are we going to do? I need to stay asleep for more than three hours at a time."

"Ooh. Ooh, I know!" I ran into the living room and fetched our His and Hers lightweight mini down comforters. I grabbed some clothespins and stood on the bed and clipped the comforters onto the cardboard. Tucker gingerly stepped up on the bed with me and stuffed the downy material around the edges to completely shut out that light. "Voila!"

13.
LENA MILLER

"Knock, knock. Hello. Can I come in? It's Rosemary! I have a broccoli–spinach–onion quiche casserole for you. Hallloooo? Where are you?"

"In the bedroom, Rosemary."

"What on earth are you two doing? Looking sun-kissed and summery in a pale pink sundress, she held a pie plate balanced high in her palm like a waitress at a country café. In the other hand, she clasped a beauteous bunch of Montauk daisies.

"Problem solving." Tucker got off the bed first. "Oh, quiche and flowers! Thank you, darling Rosemary!"

"You are the best friend, Rosie. Everything smells so good. And look, we have a baby monitor now so if Tucker calls to me in the middle of the night, it will wake me up."

"Problem solving," Tucker repeated, embarrassed by his lack of autonomy.

"The new normal." Rosie raised her eyebrow, attempting to lighten the situation as she stepped around the bedside commode to wrap her daisies-carrying arm around Tucker's slight body.

"We appreciate all you do, but nothing is normal anymore. We never know when something else will change." I relieved her of the plate and daisies and arranged the flowers in a fluted vase Tucker and I had bought the day we spotted the Black-capped Chickadee in Homer, Alaska.

Rosemary slumped into one of our kitchen chairs, defeated. "I don't know what to do. I don't know what to say. I don't want to offend you. I'm sorry. I'm tired too, ya know?"

"Oh god, I'm so sorry. I didn't mean it like that. We appreciate you so much, Rosemary," I flushed with resentment at the thought of what the drug-addled doctor had wrought on my family and friends. "We just found out that Dr. Ramon was brought up on charges of operating under the use of alcohol and had a history of felony crack cocaine possession."

"So, how the hell is he still in practice?"

"Because of institutional cover-ups. One doctor protects the next. Their boards protect them all."

Tucker enchanted us with a concert - Barrett Strong's "Oh, I Apologize" segueing into John Mayer's "Rosie." Sick or not, he was a charmer. This was a song of thanks to Rosemary. Socrates skipped in, piping in on the chorus like a backup singer. He sniffed around, looking at Rosemary with beggar's eyes. She unfastened her Mary Poppins purse and procured a small paper bag. "Socrates' portion. Here, boy." Lucky dog to have such loving humans. And us, him.

"Angela, Tucker is pale and gaunt, his face is stricken with pain, but my god, his beautiful soul shines through it all," Rosemary gushed about my husband.

"He is amazing. Rosemary, I know you go out of your way to help us, and you have your own life to live..." I spoke openly. Tucker and I were transparent with each other. Hard to keep secrets in a small house.

"No, don't even. You're my family."

"I have a favor to ask."

"What?"

"I'm going to spend less time at the store, like, maybe no time. I do the ordering from home now. Tucker fell and broke his toe last week. After that I decided to make changes."

"Oh, no, so sorry to hear that, Tucker. What kind of changes?" Rosemary shifted uncomfortably.

"We're dropping the lawsuit. The defense attorney is unscrupulous. They portray Tucker as a man who *dabbled* in life. They lie to invalidate who he is. It's too traumatic for him, and Anthony and Dr. Hollifield advised us there's no way to win this case. The medical-legal system is engineered to protect doctors.

"We're getting the bathtub replaced with a walk-in version, so Tucker doesn't have to step up into it. And I bought a treadmill, so I don't need to leave the house to run."

"You're just going to be a shut-in?"

"I'm staying close by Tucker to take care of him." *Wow. A shut-in?*

"How will you get groceries?"

"I order online."

Rosemary and I spoke privately while Tucker was out of the room. In order to remain mobile, he walked eighty times around the house daily no matter how much it hurt. He never missed a lap. He began in the kitchen, ambled down one hall and then the other, reversed when he got to the master bedroom, and looped around into the living room and back to the start. He missed his routine that morning because the bathroom carpenter was there.

"Hire someone for in-home help."

"Rosemary, I did. She ended up filming us and stealing from us. My sleep is interrupted by listening to see if Tucker is okay. Sometimes I'm up three times a night with him. I crawl in bed and the mattress sucks me in like quicksand. Really. Sometimes I lie there for two hours before I can rouse myself to eat, brush my teeth, or even get up to check on him when I want."

"You have to take care of yourself, Angie. A car can't run without fuel."

"Easier said than done. I need to hire someone full time at the store. That's where you come in."

"I love the store, but I'm too busy with my real estate business..."

"Of course, I wouldn't ask you. What do you think of this idea: Lena Miller."

"Madeleine's mom? That Lena Miller?" She bent down to rub Socrates' ears, confused.

"Yes."

"Has she expressed interest?"

"No. I haven't seen her since my parents' going away to Costa Rica party."

Tucker re-entered the kitchen on his loop-de-loops in time to hear her question. "It's another one of Angela's wild hairs. She is convinced that Lena needs a purpose and that working at Bean There might provide that for her."

"You know what? This is one of your *saner* wild hairs. That – wow - this could work. You want me to go see her with you?"

"Bingo."

"Done. I have a favor to ask of you, too."

"Of course! What can we do for you?"

Rosemary looked at Tucker, who was on another loop around the house. "Jack heard you were not feeling well. He'd like to come by and see you. Both of you," she nodded at me.

"I don't know," Tucker replied apprehensively., "I don't like people seeing me like this and I don't want Angela to be uncomfortable."

"It's fine with me, Tucker. You were good friends. It's kind of him to reach out. I don't mind."

"Great. Okay if he comes over now?" Rosemary wasted no time!

"Wow. A page right out of the Madeleine and Jared handbook. Smooth move, Rosemary."

Socrates met Jack at the door and dropped his well-loved, well-chewed orange Frisbee at his feet. In response to the dog's joyful yelps, Jack scratched behind his ears.

"Socrates! Long time, no see! Go get it, boy." He sheepishly whispered to me, "I apologize, Angie. It had nothing to do with you. You're a goddess. It was my issues. I didn't feel good enough for you.

I'm glad you got a man worthy of you. HEY, man!" He clasped Tucker on the back. "Great to see you, man."

I must say, it was good to see the man with whom I'd shared three years of my life. It reminded me I hadn't been a complete fool. Jack has many commendable qualities. He played two competitive games of chess with Tucker, unphased by the way the mayor grabbed his side and got up and stretched every few minutes. The men communicated differently than we did.

"How are the jingles, Jack?"

"The jingles are jolly."

"How is the French cow, Jack?"

"The cow's name is Molly."

"Does the cow have a friend, Jack?"

"Molly now has a best friend named Polly."

Tucker slid his queen into a position supported by a knight so Jack's king could not capture the queen and had nowhere to run. "Checkmate, mate." Seeing Tucker with a friend after months of seclusion soothed me. While the boys were busy, Rosie and I planned a visit to the Millers'.

On Saturday at ten a.m., we knew exactly where we would find Lena Miller -- tending to the gardens that grace every side of her house. My heart sped up when I saw her familiar form, just as she always was and would be in my memory forever onward, a radiant petite brunette, wearing denim overalls with the buckles unclasped, dangling to her ankles.

Lena Miller was known for elaborate and showy, yet tasteful, gardens. Lush translucent pink and white roses greeted us at the gate. Wavy flower hedges packed with yellow daffodils, lavender lilies, and white star flowers guided our way back. An ornamental brass chime tinkled a cheery tune in concert with a burbling waterfall. Cheeps and chirps from birds beckoned us in.

"This is Spotty Joe Pye Weed." *Who is Spotty Joe,* I wondered. *He sounds shady.* "They bloom in August and September and provide hollow stems for wild bees. Do you remember helping me and

Madeleine plan the spikey black cohosh, hyssop-leaved Boneset, and these red maple and winterberry bushes that have taken over the place?"

"I could never forget the hyssop-leaved Boneset," Rosie said with so much seriousness that I laughed. I transitioned the giggles into a lovely recollection.

"Nor can I ever forget the sweet scent of honeysuckle. Lena's luscious honeysuckle garden. Oh, it's so good to be home."

"I don't see you girls… ladies… enough. It does me good to be around you. Keeps Madeleine's memory alive. Did I show you what Pete did? He designed a cedar wood garden plaque with one of her favorite poems on it." Pete, Lena's brother, Madeleine's favorite uncle, a witty man who loved tapdancing, was a master craftsman who built some of the finest new houses on the Cape. We read the words hung on a four-foot post planted in the middle of roses in the backyard.

Upon Their Breathless Shadows

A littered walk of fallen dreams, an ashcan of shattered hope, street side revolutionaries, selling legal dope.

One can pull oneself up by the bootstraps, and try their best to cope, or find a coiled cordage and hang oneself with silken rope.

Felled dreams during the depression, nuclear threats, and corporate greed, made mulch of many gardens of industry, turned blooming accomplishments to seed.

For each step forward through the breech, imperious roadblocks do impede, but crafty, unfettered manacles rarely supersede people's innate, blazing drive to succeed.

So fashion tight those laces, lift high your fallen head,
Though weary, aim to find a reason to rouse yourself from bed.
Brave ancestors before us toiled from birth till they were dead.
Upon their breathless shadows we endure, we buoy, we tread.
Written by Madeleine Miller, aged 19

Your Memory is our blessing

Neither Rosemary nor I had ever read this poem Madeleine wrote not long before she hung herself. We were dumbstruck. Our dear, sweet friend, knowing that her own end was at hand, wrote this piece of poetry full of such depth and wisdom, encouraging those who could endure *to* endure. The three of us wiped our wet eyes and retreated to the house for lemonade.

We found Ty at the kitchen table assembling one of Madeleine's puzzles, just like the old days. Lena snapped puzzle edges into place like she meant business. She had come a long way since I saw her last, but still she was haunted. Ty warmed up nachos with the works for us. The three of us gabbed with a communal candor that sprang from a long history.

Just as I was ready to present my proposition, Lena jumped up. "Girls, I mean, *ladies*, I found something fun when I organized the closets." She disappeared in a flash and returned with what resembled two mops held over her head. She pumped the blue-and-white pompoms Madeleine had worked her magic with as cheer squad leader. Her enthusiasm was bittersweet.

"How did your cheer go?" Lena was eager to relive those moments.

Four of us had run for cheer squad together. We three girls and Lew, whose family moved back to Singapore after graduation and before Madeleine got sick. Madeleine and Lew went on to be cheerleaders, while Rosemary and I made track team. Madeleine was slighter and less physically powerful than us. She had spirit to spare though and cheered for all our athletes as though her life depended on it. If only her cheering had been returned to her one hundredfold.

Rosemary and I each accepted one pompom that Lena offered in her outstretched hand. Ty stopped chewing Nachos and swallowed unpulverized sharp pieces of chips.

Rosie started us out: "Ready?"

"Okay!" I responded to the call. *What else could I do?*

Then together:

I'm Maddie, I'm Rosie, I'm Angie, I'm Lew, and when you vote for us for cheerleader, here's what we're gonna do.

We'll kick off all the football games with North Yarmouth cheers.

We pantomimed a football game: the kickoff, long pass and score.

And make our senior experience the best of all years!

If it's basketball that's your sport

Here we mimicked a basketball game: dribbling, stealing, shooting.

We'll be there on the basketball court!

If baseball is your game,

Here, of course, we acted out a baseball game: the pitch, connect, then holding one hand up above our eyes and turning our heads as if to follow the home-run hit,

W'll cheer you straight to the Hall of Fame!

We'd like to change the subject, but we're running out of time, so, listen very closely to our last and final rhyme:

If you're gonna vote for cheerleader, here's what you ought to do: Vote for..."

Lena nudged Ty to stand up and they both joined in with us -

Maddie and Rosie and Angie and Lew!

Ty was deep in his memory bank. "Remember, Madeleine started the cheer with a round-off cartwheel."

"Then I repeated that." Rosemary was time-traveling, too.

"And I did a round-off but added a flip-flop." Me three.

"Finally, Lew walked out on his hands, lowered himself down from a walkover into splits, also ending with the overhead V," Rosie finished, describing the sequence for us.

Lena sat down hard on the kitchen chair and wept from a bottomless well. Ty embraced her from behind, his arms crossing her chest. I noticed they had aged more rapidly than my folks.

Heartache is a ravager. I wondered how many times this scene was replayed.

"I'm sorry, girls. Sometimes it's helpful to reminisce, but other times the wound is so raw and flashbacks so immense I collapse. We've tried therapy, medication, (which caused other problems), support groups, gardening. I keep hoping time will soften the sorrow, but it doesn't. I have nightmares that my zeal to heal my daughter caused her harm."

"Oh, no, Lena. Madeleine loved and adored you." Living in that house must be so hard.

"There's nothing to apologize about. It was a terrible situation," Rosemary added.

"I'm thrilled to see you both. I don't want you to be strangers and think I break down daily. Fill us in on your lives." And so, we did, with awareness that with each accomplishment we shared, the Millers mentally checked off a list inside their heads about what Madeleine would have done and who *she* would have become. Madeleine was forever frozen in time as the innocent she was.

Ty reheated the Nachos, and we polished them off with surprising gusto. Grief can stoke an appetite, that's for sure. Many couples get divorced after the death of a child, but the Millers, so far, withstood the life-altering pressures together. When I told them about Tucker, the bad outcome from hernia surgery, and the deleterious changes to my life, Lena was distraught. She was like a second mother to me. Living so close, Madeleine and I were like cousins on a kibbutz.

"Oh, dear, Angela. What can we do to help? Anything. Ty and I are here for you night and day."

Well, now that you ask... "There is something. It's a big favor. It might be helpful to both of us."

Rosemary, the town crier, blurted out, "Angela needs help at the bookshop. She was wondering if you might be interested in working there. It pays pretty well."

"The bookshop was mine and Madeleine's. You were the first person I thought of." Suddenly this seemed like the stupidest idea I'd ever had. My mind wandered mid-sentence out of anxiety as I wondered If Jack would feed Tucker on time before Tucker got shaky and weak.

"I've never worked retail. I read, but I'm no expert on literature."

Ty spun around from the sink where he was elbow deep in sudsy water, "But you're great with people. This is a wonderful opportunity to help Angela and continue on Madeleine's legacy."

"Plus, it will just be temporary, right?" Lena wanted to know.

"I don't know. I can't see past the nose on my face." I thought of my newly imposed lockdown with Tucker and his ever-changing non-normal needs. And my fatigue. "There's a weekly event called Living Stories. People in the community tell the story of their lives, as if they wrote a memoir. I have a sense you'd connect with this, Lena. You're so attuned to people. It would be an honor to share this precious part of my life with you, but I don't want to force you into anything. Bean There helps me deal with the loss of Madeleine. Maybe it will for you, too."

"Also, she really needs a break. I'm worried about her." Rosemary made a short, poignant case.

Lena picked up a cardboard jigsaw piece and snapped it in the middle of the puzzle, bringing into focus the face of an elephant. She looked down at the pompoms with moist eyes. "Maddie would love me to be involved in your bookstore. Who knows, I might too."

14.
THE SCRIPT

"Hello, North Yarmouth Grief and Support Talk Line. This is Angela. What's your name?"

"Justine."

"Hi Justine. What's going on tonight?"

"I feel that the world is covered in a dark energy. I don't know who I can trust anymore."

"That's a big statement. See if you can break it down-- what does this mean to you?"

"The world, politics..."

"Let's start with one thing at a time."

"But that's just it! There's not one thing. There's a pile of human rights and values being knocked out and before we can catch one, another freedom is stripped away. Did you know that they deregulated medical devices?"

"No. I didn't."

"That's what I mean. How do you keep track of it all? Where are the checks and balances? My son died from medical malpractice. A device was used that never should have been approved. It got passed as a 501 K predicate. We don't need fewer regulations in medicine. We need to hold these crooks responsible for murdering healthy people. The surgery was supposed to be minor, but boom, he was strong and healthy, only eighteen years old, but was killed."

"I'm so sorry to hear about your son. When did you lose him?"

"Ten years ago. Angela, I'm exhausted from this world. Exhausted."

"Me, too."

"You don't like it either?"

"I try not to talk about my own political views on the talk line. I'm exhausted because our phones are blowing up and a medical device harmed someone I love."

"Damn, sister. You too? I never called a talk line before. I didn't know if it was appropriate but I'm going out of my mind tonight."

"This is what we're here for. Thank you for letting me know about the medical devices. I'll have to look that up."

"You're welcome. I just needed to tell someone, that's all."

"Justine, I'm here Tuesdays and Wednesdays from 6:00 to midnight. Call anytime you need."

"I probably will. I'm so tired of ducking hard balls being slammed at my head."

"What are you going to do when we hang up?"

"I don't know. I like to dance. I can put on some music."

"What are you going to put on?"

"Maybe Talking Heads."

"'Psycho Killer'?"

"You got it."

"Call again if you need me."

"Bye."

Click.

"Hello, North Yarmouth Grief and Support Talk Line. This is Angela. What's your name?"

"Kiara. Hey, thanks for taking my call."

"Sure. What's going on tonight, Kiara?"

"Umm... I'm fed up. I'm losing hope."

"I'm sorry to hear that. What's happening?"

"What's happening is that our leaders seem determined to ruin our air, water, national parks, and kill off the arts. Do you know medical malpractice is a lead cause of death in the U.S.? I have an eighteen-month-old. How will I explain to that innocent boy that our world is run by greed? Sometimes I regret having him. Hello? Angela, are you there?"

"Yes, I'm here. I'm really sorry for your pain. I know about the medical malpractice. We get a lot of calls like this. It helps people to get involved in helping others."

"What, that's it? I call a hotline, and this is what I get? It sounds like you're reciting something like a robot. This talk line has a good reputation. If you don't even believe what you're saying, how am I going to? And how am I going to get involved in helping others when I'm busy running after my little guy and trying to get him to eat his vegetables and poop in the toilet?"

"Kiara, I have the same concerns as you about the future. I apologize for not sounding genuine. You struck a painful chord with me. I have to do something to be of help, which is why I volunteer at this severely understaffed crisis line. Maybe I shouldn't do it anymore."

"Well, now you sound more like a human. Just talk to me, Angela. Be *real* with me."

"Kiara. I'm a mess. Figure out what you can do. Everyone is different. Take care of yourself and your family first. I can't imagine how hard it'd be if I had a toddler."

"I want to do more. I need to. How long are the volunteer shifts at the severely understaffed North Yarmouth Grief and Support Talk Line?"

"Shortest one, two hours a week."

"You gonna teach me to read your scripts and sound robotic?"

"We teach you to listen and find out what matters to someone. The training is two weeks long."

"Well, I can do that. Uh-huh. How do I get the information?"

"I'll transfer you to Geneviève's voicemail. Leave your email and phone number. I'm here Tuesdays and Wednesdays from 6:00 p.m. to midnight. You can call me anytime."

"Angela, *you* gonna be calling me."

"Probably! Hey, Kiara, who's your favorite singer?"

"Patsy Cline."

"You feel like singing "Crazy" with me?"

"Pssh. You on, girl." We sang.

Carla tapped me on the shoulder. "We have a reporter on the line. He wants to talk to the manager."

"Kiara, I hope to meet you someday."

"Oh, you shall, Angela, you shall."

Click.

"Hello, this is Angela. I'm the manager here."

"Hello, Angela. I'm Patrick Nunsun from the *North Yarmouth Post.* I'd like to do a story about your services."

"What kind of story, Patrick? What's the angle? There's always an angle."

"For one thing, I'm wondering how calls may have increased over the past three years. Sort of to get a read on the public temperature."

"I don't know if you can read public temperature by interviewing me."

"Have calls gone up in the past years?"

"Significantly."

"Do you have numbers?"

"Yes."

"I'd like to schedule an interview with you."

"Do I get final approval?"

"No. We don't do that sort of thing."

"Well then, no. I've seen reporters get facts wrong too often."

"Look, I'm a reputable..."

"No, Patrick. I made myself clear. I'm not having any false information printed about the center. Final approval, or no interview. Take it or leave it, but I have to get back to my phones."

"Okay. I'll make an exception."

"Fine, but if you're going to interview someone, this should be the rule. I'll transfer you to my voicemail. Leave your details. I'll call tomorrow to set up a time."

"You drive a hard bargain, Angela."

"Not at all. I'm just reality based. I run a grief talk line, Mr. Nunson. I'm here Tuesdays and Wednesdays from 6:00 p.m. to midnight. Call me any time."

Click.

For the next year, Tucker and I found a way to thrive through the cracks during the quiet of night, a time that incites a surge in creative spirit; the hallowed stillness in the crate of time when the sun warms her subjects in other lands and the moon keeps a watch as a loving parent does. The beauteous bit in between the rise and fall of the light is the night. Frogs croak, spring peepers creep from ponds, and judgments, assumptions, and expectations wane with the waning moon. Hope, freedom, and the thirst for boundless imagination expand with her waxing. The middle of the night was our time to be a couple without hindrance or restraint. *A couple of what is the question.* Tucker did a spot-on Groucho Marx imitation when he posed that inquiry.

"In my head I hear the beating of Mashpee Wampanoag drums," he said.

"What is that?" I wanted to know what was in his head.

He showed me videos of Mashpee Wampanoag Powwows. "Wow, powerful." We held our own ceremonies in honor of these brave, displaced souls. There is so much suffering in our world, so much cruelty and unfairness. Tucker and I were now a hodge-podge of cynicism and idealism. Art and music uplifted us.

We conceived a joint project we called "Around the World in 200 Days." Tucker's part was to study and play world music. My task was to find literature, poems, or essays from each of the 195 nations on the planet. We invested ourselves with pure love. This was our way of continuing to travel and expand our understanding of diversity and divine humanness during our years of being grounded due to the mesh mess, or the *god damn fucking mesh mess*, as Tucker called it.

Both of us spent a copious amount of time researching and taking notes on each country and its unique artistic contributions. A time such as these tender night sessions in the post-sunset predawn swath of velvety blackness gave birth to our growth as a dialectical doublet who dabbled in whatever we were drawn to. The only limit was pain.

And pain is a spiteful hellcat, challenged by love, subordinate to none.

"Hello, North Yarmouth Grief and Support Talk Line. This is Angela. What's your name?"

"Taylor. I can't do it anymore."

"What?"

"You know, the whole thing."

"I see. I'm sorry to hear that."

"Yeah."

"Okay."

"Care. I can't keep caring."

"Uh-huh."

"About anyone, anything."

"I hear you."

"Yeah. I'm done."

"If that's how it is, you have to do what you have to do."

"It's too much."

"It can be."

"Our country, the world...."

"Go on, I'm listening."

"No more news, no more activism. I'm cutting off."

"Sounds like what you need."

"Maybe I'll still help with the scouts."

"All right, I can see that."

"Maybe I'll make some phone calls to my Senators."

"If that feels right."

"We're supposed to call by tomorrow. Have you called yet? Do you do that sort of thing?"

"I do. I have."

"I missed them today. I had decided to unplug."

"Well, some days are like that."

"I'll be sure to call tomorrow."

"Okay.'

"Thank you."

"You're welcome. I'm here Tuesdays and Wednesdays from 6:00 p.m. to midnight. Call me any time."

Click.

"Hello, North Yarmouth Grief and Support Talk Line. This is Angela. What's your name?"

"Ed."

"Hi, Ed. "What's going on for you tonight?"

"I want to do more."

"Like what?"

"I have skin cancer. I was in remission for three years, but it's back and it's worse. I want to do more in the time I have left, you know, set things up for my kids long-term."

"Oh, I see. I'm sorry to hear that."

"Is it okay if I just unload on you for a bit?"

"Yes. It's okay."

"Can you hear me? Am I talking loudly enough?"

"Uh-huh."

"I get weak and it's hard to project."

"I can hear you."

"Sometimes I can push through a day and other times I just have to rest. I can't do anything. Have to stay in bed."

"If that's how it is, you have to do what you have to do."

"It's hard to be sick, Angela. Very hard."

"It can be."

"I... I..." (Gasp)

"I'm here. I'm listening."

"I'm going to have to hang up soon. I'm getting fatigued."

"Sounds like what you need."

"Do you know what it feels like to want to do more but not be able to?"

"I do."

"I thought today might be different." Sigh.

"Well, some days are like that, Ed."

"You're very understanding. Maybe we can talk another time."

"Okay."

"Thank you."

"You're welcome. I'm here Tuesdays and Wednesdays from 6:00 p.m. to midnight. Call me any time."

Click.

"Hi, Britta, what's up?" Britta was my star student during the last big training. "Are you getting comfortable working the hotline?"

"Angela, how did you come up with this script? It's brilliant. So minimal. So powerful."

"What script?"

Britta looks at the notes she scribbled. "What? I see. Okay. Uh-huh. I hear you. If that's how it is, you have to do what you have to do. It can be. Oh, yes. Sounds like what you need. All right, I can see that. If that feels right. I do. Well, some days are like that. Okay. You're welcome."

"Britta, no, no, I... I just... I just listen... I do what comes naturally. Each conversation is unique."

"You just said THIS in the past two calls in a row. EXACTLY, Angie."

I held up my finger. "Hang on a second, Brit."

"Hello, North Yarmouth Grief and Support Talk Line. This is Angela. What's your name?"

"It's me, Angie."

"Robby, what's wrong?"

"It's my dad. He had a heart attack."

"Oh, I see. I'm so sorry to hear that."

"I feel like it's my fault, you know because of the stress with my injury and everything in the past years. Can you hang on a sec?"

"Okay."

"Mom, I'm on the phone. I'll be right there! You still there?"

"Uh-huh."

"I'm so worried about him. I feel like I want to scream, Angie. I don't know what to do. I wake up in the middle of the night and have to go out for air. I feel like I'm being smothered."

Angela looked desperately at Britta and motioned for the paper.

"You have to do what you have to do."

"The moon is so comforting to me. The crescent is beautiful."

"Yes, it is... can be."

Britta and I stared at each other, stunned.

"Mom says I should learn to sleep through the night, but the night air is so refreshing."

Britta silently forms the words, "Sounds like what you need."

"Sounds like what you need."

"I'm going to have to go. Mom's yelling for me to get off the phone."

"All right.

Britta sat down, shaking her head in disbelief.

"I want to write a letter to my dad and tell him how I feel," Robby said.

Britta nods to Angie. "If that feels right."

"Today was long day, Angie. If felt like it was a week long."

"Well, some days are like that."

"Maybe I can call earlier tomorrow so we can talk longer."

"Okay."

"You're the only one who totally gets me, Angie. Thank you so much."

"You're welcome."

Click.

"Weird! On paper this might look impersonal and caring, but your intonation and investment makes this script work." Britta looked spooked. I didn't know what to say. "May I?" Britta motioned to the paper. I nodded and handed the scribbled notes to her.

15.
THE WHISPER BENCH

We watched *Jeopardy!* from bed, curled around each other. There were no fist pumps or wild conga dances, but the game still engaged us.

Who is Scarlett O'Hara?

What is Uruguay?

What is paella?

What is Hydra?

Who is Daniel Ellsberg?

The Final Jeopardy category was "Great Lakes." Tucker said he was betting everything. He barely seemed to hear the answer: *An 1855 poem mentions this Native American term for the one Great Lake not known to us today by a Native American word."*

"The Whisper Bench."

"What is *Gitiche Gumee?* Come on, you'd know this one. The answer was, 'An 1855 poem mentions this Native American...'"

"My question is when can we go to the Whisper Bench?"

"Tucker, you want to go there?"

"Yes."

"You haven't been out of the house in two years."

"I want to go. Just me and you. My last hurrah."

"Don't say that."

"There's something I want to tell you there."

"You can tell me anything here."

"Angela."

"Do you want me to drive us?"

"Amtrak. Bus. I'll go in a wheelchair."

"It will be hours on public transportation. It'll wear you out."

His look was certain.

"Okay, then. When do you want to go?"

"Tuesday. Slow day."

"All right. I'll set everything up. You know, you don't have to go anywhere."

"Is this your reverse psychology?"

"No, Tucker. I just want you to be comfortable. You don't have to do anything or push yourself."

His look was firm. "I've been thinking about this for months. We're going to go on an outing. I have to say, I'm excited. It's been a long time."

The bench is on the West Side of the park near the 79-81 transverse road through the park, next to Central Park West. There's a subway stop at 81st and Central Park West in front of the American Museum of Natural History.

Robby's father was doing better, so, I asked Robby to accompany us to help me with Tucker physically. He stayed back so the mayor and I could spend time alone. When Tucker was healthy, our monthly Manhattan forays always included visits to the MET, History Museum, MOMA, or one of the many cultural treasures in the city, but on this day, just getting to the bench and getting Tucker to Brooklyn in one piece was my *raison d'être*.

Sitting on the subway in his wool beanie, crocheted scarf, and hiking shoes, Tucker looked like a child playing the role of an eighty-year-old in a play. His debilitating physical state, hunched shoulders, excruciating movements, pain, and pallor had aged him. His feet casually crossed at his ankles like little boy in conjunction with those big honest eyes of his, magnified through his eyeglass lenses, generated an air of innocence and wonder. He was so vulnerable it was shattering to me, but I needn't have worried about Tucker. True to his spirit, he conversed with everyone in his line of mobility. His hands, warm in puffy protective knit mittens, waved in the air as he pointed out landmarks to a group of Japanese teenagers in The Big Apple for the first time. A busker with a guitar got on the train and sat in the seat opposite Tucker. They talked about music for an hour. He handed Tuck the guitar and mittenless, he played the blues, man.

I sat in between Tucker and Robby. Robby squeezed my hand whenever he sensed I needed support or shook from adrenaline or the cold though I couldn't differentiate which was which.

Robby pushed Tucker in the wheelchair through the lush park, past Shakespeare's Garden where tulips, crocuses, daffodils, fritillaries, anemones, hellebores, and roses beamed goodwill out to us, and on to the bench. Tuck assimilated everything he saw with awe and guilelessness as if it was his first time on this planet and the final time he would be well enough to make this sojourn.

Tucker leaned his head back and watched a bold red cardinal circle overhead. "I'm in the world but not of it. I long to soar like a bird, high above it."

"That's beautiful. Who said that?" Robby asked.

"I did," Tucker replied.

The bench is a place so special to us, I half expected to see our names engraved on the plaque. With Tucker situated at one end, I sat on the other and looked over at him with unconditional love. I fought to keep my eyes dry.

Tucker whispered to me first. "I want to die," he simply said.

"I know, my love. I know."

"I mean, it's time. Soon. I want to plan for it. I hope you will support me."

"I hope my interest in the right to die hasn't influenced you."

"Why would you hope that? Isn't that the point?"

"Well, has it?"

A family of four glided onto the bench in between us, eating fat, salty pretzels, and chattering about the day. Tucker and I patiently awaited their departure.

"I would have come to this conclusion on my own. If you were contrary, angry at me, blamed me, or saw me as selfish, it would increase my distress, and I have enough on my crowded plate of indignities as it is. I don't think..."

I went to sit next to him. He cleared his throat. I offered him water, concerned he was choking. He refused the drink and tried again, choking on the emotionality of it. "I don't think Sheba would have approved. She would have fought me."

This was the first time I heard Tucker intimate any adversity in relation to her.

"Does her imagined disapproval weigh on you? Perhaps she'd have understood as I do."

"It doesn't impact me other than that I'm grateful for you. My feeling of guilt, such as it is, has to do with having a preference for you over her. I vowed to love you equally, but I've gotten to know you in such a deeply profound way. I love you more. I betrayed Sheba."

Oh!

Platitudes feverishly swirled through my head. The word-fast training came in handy at moments like this. I let his words be, as they were, without the need to cloud them by my discomfort. After their impact had time to settle, I said, "Sheba loved you fully. Now I do. You are a special person, Tucker. You love with your whole heart as much as you can. About your whisper confession, do you want me to fight you on this? Is this why you bring up Sheba?"

"God, no. I'm clear on this."

"You're not a burden to me. I would be happy living in a cardboard box with you."

"Yes, but I'm worse every day. I'm worried about having a stroke or heart attack due to pain and stress. I don't want to end up in a medical institution. I hope I didn't wait too long."

Robby checked on us. "You two look tired. Tucker's parents will be here soon to meet us. We should go now."

Brynn and Michael were overjoyed to see their boy. His mother took his face in her hands and double-kissed his cheeks until his father had to nearly pull her off. Tucker was so tired that he lay down on a bench. Robby suggested again that it was time to go.

"We'll come see you soon, son," Michael promised, but I knew they wouldn't see each other again. I think they did, too. Tucker told them about his choice so they wouldn't be shocked. After a weeklong visit and many tears, his parents grew to understand his rational, gut-wrenching decision. They saw him put up the cardboards and take sleep medication, but still struggle to sleep due to the structural harm. Every step, every breath, every bite, agonizing. It's one thing to visit for a few hours; being present for the unrelenting trials gave them a realistic perspective.

Tucker and I laid our heads together as the train whizzed through a New York and New England we'd loved collectively, and soon I'd love singularly in memory of my husband. When he dozed off. I delicately took his mittened hand in mine and whispered, "And I vowed to embrace Sheba as part of us. This is the first time I envy her because she had you until her end."

When we got home, we met in the kitchen. I wrote a poem for Tucker, and as turnabout is fair play, he wrote one for me. I read him mine first.

I WISH YOU WINGS

To Tucker

I wish you wings, to fly, to soar
Beyond your body, outside earth's doors.
I wish you hope, to cope, to roar

Against the limits you so abhor.

I wish you safety, peace of mind,
All the love you can find.
I wish you nectar to cleanse worldly grime,
And liberty to renew your soul in time.

I wish you well, dear husband, be strong.
I wish you peace: short-term, eternity-long.
I ache to hear your freedom song.
I wish you well, dear Tucker, be strong.

The answer is: the reason I was born.
The question: what is to love you with all my heart?
Forever, Angela

    Then he read me his.

LOVE POOLS

To Angela

Punishing winds.
Plans snuffed out.
Visions blown away.
Infernos rage
As we turn the page
On an unforeseen brand-new day.

Of this I'm sure,
I understand nothing of life,
But who I am amidst the rubble.
Try as I may, if I had my say,
I'd have steered clear of loss and trouble.

Luck reigns or wanes in various ways,
Perhaps in the most strident or gentile lives.
When death comes to me soon,
Know you still light up the room
And in dreams birds soar and dive.

There are no set rules.
The heart tears, love pools,
But we move forward anyway.

I only regret that I had to leave you.
I cherish you beyond the known and unknown,
Forever, my dear.
Love, Tucker..

"Hello, North Yarmouth Grief and Support Talk Line. This is Angela. What's your name?"

"Anne..."

"Bill..."

"Chris..."

"Duarte..."

"Erin..."

"Fia..."

"Gregg..."

"Hamlin."

"Irma."

"Ahhhhhh!"

"Wake up, Ang. What's wrong? You had another nightmare."

"Nothing, Tucker. It's okay. Go back to sleep."

16.

FINAL LULLABY

We met on a Tuesday night, got married on a Tuesday night, and Tuesday nights were our date nights. Here we were again. Tuesday. Night. Midnight. A knock on the door made me jump two feet in the air like a Staffordshire Terrier.

"Hi Geneviève. Hi Rosemary. Thank you for coming."

Of course Geneviève petted my arm, which was meant to comfort me, but my face flushed. I had to hold back a scream. *It's Tuesday night. Date night. I don't want him to leave.*

We knew of a man whose beloved wife of twenty-seven years had to end her life alone without the comfort of her husband so that he wouldn't be put in legal jeopardy. Tucker and I considered all of the possible ramifications of his actions. We confided in two people besides Brynn and Michael: Geneviève and Rosemary. Tucker wrote and recorded clear testimony that stated his wishes. Rosemary would film the event. She and Geneviève would be witnesses.

None of us was willing to let Tucker die alone.

"Where's Tucker?"

I nodded towards the bedroom. I assumed that the look in my eyes conveyed that neither of us was doing well. Rosemary sighed, gave me a lingering hug, and walked into his room first.

"Hi. Tucker." He held his hand out to her. It was covered in hives.

She sat on the bed. "Friend zone?"

He smiled. The Tucker eye crinkle. "Friends," wisped out of his mouth.

"Hi, Tucker." He tapped the bed for Geneviève to sit. Unsure of deathbed etiquette, the two of them were quiet.

"Don't all talk at once. You're not on a word fast, are you? I'm still alive, ya know. You can talk to me."

"How are you, buddy?"

"I'm scared, in horrible pain, and worried for Angela. Promise me you'll take care of her."

That did it. I left the room so he wouldn't see me break down. Doubled over, my face looked purple in the reflection from the stainless-steel stove. Geneviève bear-hugged me from the back.

"I'm sad he has to hasten his death. His life was stopped mid-leap, and he had to endure years of suffering. I'm devasted that I will exist in a world without Tucker."

Tucker chose our seventh wedding anniversary to leave. In his trademark cursive that rolls like summer waves, he had written, "Choosing to end my life before I fully lose my full autonomy is an act of self-compassion. I believe in the right to choose to leave my body when life becomes intolerable, which mine has been for years."

I planned to sing "The Parting Glass," a Scottish traditional folk song, as his final lullaby. I visualized him closing his eyes as his breathing, which had been labored for years, stopped. But visualizations are wishes, and wishes are not always answered. Life has its own design. A ghastly noise like a foghorn came from Tucker's room. Socrates barked and whined, pawing to get in. "RAAAAAWWWWWW" from the bedroom. "Wooooff" from the yard. Then a thud. Sweat poured down my face. We rushed to him like a football squad tearing for a tackle.

He was down.

Man down.

Tucker.

Tucker.

Tucker.

He clutched his chest.

Couldn't speak.

"Heart attack. Stroke," someone said.

Tucker.

He wanted to die.

Didn't want to live in any more pain.

Didn't even get a choice in death.

I loved him so much I would have ended his life then and there instead of having him suffer anymore. I was ready to smother him. Choke him. Set the house on fire. He was gone. I knew it. Mesh, terror, and pain killed him. I hurled myself on top of him. Then everything went black.

"Tucker!"

"Of all the money that e'er I had
I spent it in good company
And all the harm I've ever done
Alas, it was to none but me
And all I've done for want of wit
To memory now I can't recall
So fill to me the parting glass
Good night and joy be to you all
So, fill to me the parting glass
And drink a health whate'er befalls
Then gently rise and softly call
Good night and joy be to you all
Of all the comrades that e'er I had
They're sorry for my going away
And all the sweethearts that e'er I had
They'd wish me one more day to stay
But since it fell into my lot

That I should rise and you should not
I'll gently rise and softly call
Good night and joy be to you all
Fill to me the parting glass
And drink a health whate'er befalls
Then gently rise and softly call
Good night and joy be to you all
La ra la ra la la
La lala lala la la
La ra lala la la
La la la lala la la
But since it fell into my lot
That I should rise and you should not
I'll gently rise and softly call
Good night and joy be to you all
So, fill to me the parting glass
And drink a health whate'er befalls
Then gently rise and softly call
Good night and joy be to you all
Good night and joy be to you all."

Voluntarily taking one's life is stigmatized in much of the world. If you look up suicide online, first of all you will be directed to call a hotline or reach out for help. Second of all, you will be shown descriptions of people who are mentally ill, anxious and depressed, schizophrenic, bullied, alcoholics, drug abusers, and more. Tucker was none of these things. He was trapped in a body damaged so badly, there was no hope or relief, and he was progressively getting worse.

He planned his exit meticulously. He asked me to get support for myself. I did for Tucker what I'd want if faced with the same situation. I didn't encourage him, but I showed up and loved him.

As I looked around the crowded North Yarmouth Community Theatre, (the management had kindly lent me their auditorium for Tucker's Memorial), I saw a sea of friendly, familiar folks who set aside their sunny Sunday to pay respects to my beloved husband. If the position were reversed and Tucker was alive and I was dead, he would be working the room, pulling everyone into a warm embrace, bowing, and expressing gratitude for their presence, but there I sat on the stage strangely stoic as though I was competing for the world record of stolid demeanor.

Anything you feel or don't feel is okay. It's all normal. You're in shock. Just breathe. You'll get through it. I was so busy coaching myself that I didn't notice when Michael and Brynn approached. Upon sight of his grieving parents, I was overcome as if a Mack truck rolled over my chest. I wondered if I would make it alive through this day. There are no condolences strong enough for parents who outlive their children. Tucker's father extended his arm to help me get up. I heard my inner voice guide me to straighten my legs and lift myself. *Now is when you stand and hug them.* I wanted to express my condolences, say I was sorry, not to apologize, but to empathize with their loss. The words backlogged in my throat.

Brynn enveloped me in one of her famous soft lavender-scented hugs.

"He loved you so much," I said softly into her ear.

Next, Michael and I embraced.

"Tucker loved and revered you."

They set me back in my chair. I returned to the stoic zone. I sat still conserving energy to survive.

Michael sat at the piano like a king who had ascended his throne. He and Tucker's band, (Tyrone on trumpet, Angelo on bass, and Claudia, lead guitar), played Walter C. Trout's "Say Goodbye to the Blues," which was one of Tucker's favorite songs and entirely befitting of his earthly send-off. *The earth is finally taking you to a place where there ain't no more bad news.*

The service was the most musical and poetic I'd seen, perfectly befitting a man whose love and creativity touched so many. Sheba's parents were there. Saying good-bye to him was wrenching for them; they loved him like a son. The praise piled on in eulogies by friends and family.

His loving gaze made the world align and dance.
He embodies and transmitted love.
Tucker was a playful person.
His life was a song.
I will miss him forever.

Emma Boyd was not present. Ten years older, she'd always been jealous of her young, bright brother. She treated him as a child his whole life, while leaving the care of their parents to Tucker who aided Brynn when she had Pleurisy and then sepsis, and Michael when he broke an arm and leg skiing. Sometimes it's like that in families. The sadness of Emma's cumulative absence hung over the ceremony and had been a dark spot in Tucker's and his parents' hearts.

My parents flew in from their new home in Portugal. They each read a passage from *Flaubert's Correspondence with George Sand.* While they read, there wasn't a dry eye in the house. Tucker would have loved all the artistic presentations.

The next Sunday, Rosie, Geneviève, Robby, Jack, and I piled in Kieran Junior's truck and trekked up to Maine to the spot where Mary Rose's memorial was. This was the spot Tucker had asked me to spread his ashes.

I walked barefoot on the sand, closed my eyes, and spun around like I was on the top of the Austrian Alps, and whispered, *The answer is: he, a gregarious, creative, saintly presence always had a hug, kind words, and song to uplift his brethren and loved to metaphorically fly on the backs of the birds he filmed, and on me.* One by one, everyone asked, *Who is Tucker?*

Presente. May his memory be a blessing. After freeing him to the winds, we brunched at the Flap Jack Factory where we feasted on the Fisherman's Catch of the Day and shared remembrances of Tucker Boyd and his lovely, wild ways.

17.
JOHNNY

The steady roar of the waves was comforting. Our bodies acclimated to the sand and water like wearing a favorite tee shirt, soft from wear, familiar to the skin. A light drizzle fell. A young woman in jean cut-offs jogged up to Geneviève.

"Excuse me, are you Geneviève?"

"Yes, I am. Who are you?"

"Lorelei. I'm Johnny's granddaughter. I can't believe I found you, finally!"

"Johnny? *My* Johnny? Is he alive?"

"Yes, very much so. He had a stroke. We took him home to Boston to heal. He's been begging me to find you. I tried conventional means to look up your details. Grandpa said to come to the beach at noon on the solstice. My mom said you wouldn't be here, but I knew you would!" She threw her arms around Genevieve.

"Oh, honey, I'm so glad you came. How is he?"

"Come with me and see for yourself?"

18.
MAKE ME AN ANGEL

Just outside the door I heard the sweet chirp of the Robin's song signaling the swell of Spring as I nimbly catalogued month-end profits for Bean There. My mind was on the task at hand, but my heart was with Tucker. I was on my way to perfecting this dualistic existence: being fully present and wrapped in the spirit of Tucker Boyd as a foundation, a reality as sure as my breath.

The chime of the front bell alerted me that a customer had come into the shop. I peeked my head round the corner to see Kanshin, a literature professor who had made weekly forays into the store since the last Halloween, I recall, making my acquaintance as Hamlet. A man full of curiosity and knowledge about culture and the arts, he often made me laugh with his dry and dramatic wit.

"Oh, hi, Kanshin."

"That is a beautiful bird," he said, referencing the photo I'd hung over the register.

"Indeed. It's the majestic Andean Condor. My husband took it the day he proposed to me."

"Oh, I'm sorry, I didn't realize you were married."

"Widowed."

"Well, this is awkward." He squirmed as though his clothes were too tight. "I just spent six months working up my courage to ask you on a date."

"I can think of worse things to do over a blizzardy winter. Even we widows need to get out occasionally. Maybe we could take a walk sometime?" My words were accompanied by a soft smile as though I somehow needed to comfort him.

"Sure, I like walking. When?"

I shrugged my shoulders. "Now?"

"Now is my favorite time." Kanshin held me in a compassionate gaze.

"I'll lock up and get my runners on. I should let you know that a date with me won't lead anywhere. It's six months since his death and I can't ever imagine…" My voice cracked.

"How about we just go for a walk as friends. If you'd like, you can tell me about him."

"Tucker."

"Tucker. I'm a good listener. I'd also love to hear about seeing the condor and anything else you want to talk about."

"Likewise, Kanshin."

And so that's what we did. Kanshin and I took friendship walks every Tuesday for two months. He taught me about the local plants, French cinema, world literature, and his life as a first-generation American. I talked about life and travels with Tucker, his music and birding, the grief call line, gemstones, and anything I wanted. I invited Kanshin to the potlucks at the North Yarmouth Community Support Center, and we went to Broadway shows, Central Park, and shared a weekend on Martha's Vineyard. While riding the carousel I realized I was so deeply in love with Tucker that it wouldn't be right to pull another man into my life. Maybe ever.

"I'm a patient man. I don't have expectations," Kanshin said.

"I expect that someday you'll meet someone with a less complicated past. Most days I miss him so much it feels like a rubber band is tied around my waist. I struggle just to get a breath in."

"Understood. I have enjoyed your company. What are your plans now, Angela?"

"I sold the store to some friends, Lena and Ty Miller. I'm going to travel to destinations Tucker and I planned to see together, get to know other cultures, go birding. I'm learning to use his camera. My first trip is to Italy so I can use the Italian my husband and I learned together."

"Look me up when you come back. We'll get together -- as friends."

"I will, Kanshin." *But I won't. I don't plan to come back.*

I knew immediately after Tucker died what I wanted to do. My own voice was edged out by the many people, including well-meaning Rosemary, who had told me to wait a year before I made big decisions. I forced myself to stay put for eight months, longer than I should have stayed. My status quo had been annihilated long ago - beginning the day Tucker fell out of his handstand.

I sold the Derby Road house first, which we had been renting out. Rosemary was my agent. It was snatched up by a couple in the throes of empty-nest syndrome. I hoped the house would give their second act a joyous backdrop. I wondered if they would sense the spirits of Sheba, Tucker, Socrates and me within those beloved walls.

Next, the Millers officially took over Bean There, Done That. Carrying on Madeleine's vision gave them a purpose. They vowed to continue Living Story Nights. I didn't ask them to, but I'm glad that legacy lives on.

Tucker's parents took some of Tucker's instruments. It was easy to let go of most of what I owned. Furniture, rugs, plants, dishware, books, electronics. None of these items was Tucker. He's all I wanted, but he was gone. Rosemary offered to babysit my gemstones. I scanned photos from my marriage and Sheba's. Hard copies went into Rosemary's basement. I kept Tucker's glasses and his tee-shirts, which I wore to bed every night, and sometimes even all day long.

In the years he was housebound from the mesh mess, Tucker wrote stories to accompany his favorite bird photographs. It was published as a coffee table book: *Into The Boyd.* The Andean Condor graced the cover. Lena said she'd display the book at Bean There as soon as it came out.

Saying goodbye to Geneviève was sad. We built a community together. I'd imagined myself growing old in North Yarmouth and nurturing the center through layers of change. Carrie Okazaki from Minnesota came took over as vice president, now a paid position, and Kiara, who had called me out for sounding like a robot, stepped into my role as teacher and head of the volunteers. Geneviève and I watched silently as the movers delivered Tucker's piano to the center. He specified in his last will and testament that this was where he wanted it to go. After I plunked out a few notes of *The Parting Glass,* I walked out and wandered the streets in a haze until the chill forced me home.

I waited at the light for molasses minutes, slow and sticky in the Massachusetts sunshine, antsy with angst at the anticipation of what was come. Socrates lifted his head to give a yelp of delight in the early morning light on the drive to the doggie park where I took him to say farewell to his friends. Then he flopped his head back down, his eyes sorrowful from missing Tucker, his heart weak from old age, cancer, and degenerative joint disease. The same sun that shone then shone now, only just a little older and hopefully, wiser.

The *beep-de-de-dee-beep* of impatient drivers, secure inside the long line of cars piled up behind me, honked in a sort of symphony ranging from 108 to 125 decibels. The tempo alternated between Staccato and Allegro depending on the level of rashness or exasperation each motorist felt for me when I didn't immediately floor through the crosswalk the *moment* the streetlight indicated GO. It was the light and flirtatious solo blast which reminded me of

Mozart's "Horn Concerto No. 3 in E-flat Major" that brought me back to the present day.

Perhaps it was a dream that life was ever moist like a fresh tomato, ever a clear vista stretching before my legs. Ever as ever. Ever as Tucker's grin, gripping his guitar while Socrates jumped lap-high and doggie serenaded us, ever the perfect Sunday, which seemed so long ago.

On that Monday, a sweet Sunday seemed never to have been. From my car speakers, Bluesy Bonnie Raitt implored me to be an angel. I rubbed Socrates behind the ears. This turn was unexpected for a Monday. Unexpected ever, though it all made sense in the scheme of things.

Lost in the Rorschach of white-cream clouds, I heard Titanic musicians play "Autumn" defiantly, desperately, idealistically, heroically. I saw Anne Frank, shadow-living in an Amsterdam attic and scribbling, *despite everything, I really believe people are good at heart.*

I positioned my arm out the window and waved a comrade's greeting to the fellows behind me. Someday they too will miss the sudden turn of a light. Someday they too will perhaps lose the person they most love. The bluster of the day, the blunder that had steamed my way, seemed surreal, a never event. Never imagined, sanctioned, asked for, consented, needed, just, or okay. Like my perilous predecessors before me, I sighed. *Make me an angel that flies from Montgomery*, I mouthed before turning into the Vet's office where I would part with Socrates by singing him the final lullaby that I wasn't able to sing to Tucker.

After twelve years of being proprietress of my treasured bookshop, it was at last my turn to share at Living Story Night. Friends, customers, and colleagues signed a foot-high card featuring a rendition of the storefront with a portrait of me sipping tea at one of the little tables. The card requested me to share what Tucker and

I had gone through. Everyone, even Jonah Dunn, Lillian Stein, and Tami, the tattooed police officer signed the card.

Rosemary begged me not to wear one of Tucker's tee-shirts.

"How this?" I held up a peasant folk blouse with puffy sleeves that I had gotten in Romania not long before the mesh mess. It was embroidered with wine, silver, gold, and pale blue satin bands cinched at the wrists, waist, hips, and shoulders.

"Perfect! And wear the Malachite earrings from Peru."

"Yes, mam." I hated when Rosemary told me what to do, but in a world of choosing one's battles, this was not one of them. *She cares enough to impose herself. Just go with it.*

There are a multitude of stories about my life I could have told, but there was only one story I wanted to tell.

"Good evening. Thank you for coming out on this frosty evening. I'm Angela Boyd, founder and owner – now former owner - of Bean There, Done That, which..."

The crowd got up on their feet and applauded me. Tears glistened on my lashes as I searched the room for the person I wished to share this moment with, my *Anam Cara,* but he wasn't there. I motioned for the audience to sit down. If I didn't keep up the momentum, I would lose my nerve.

"Bean There, Done That is now in the capable hands of Ty and Lean Miller." I gestured for the Millers to stand and be acknowledged. They waved humbly and quickly sat back down. The local patronage knew the Millers already. Lena's first move had been to plant a triangle leaf fig tree mid-store. Its ornamental heart-shaped green and cream foliage lilted upwards to the skylight. Flanking the Ficus were rose colored ceramic pots with dark green peace lilies. Banana leaf white blooms and croton plants splayed reds, yellows, and greens like a peacock.

"It's inevitable that we're going to die. Every one of us. Yet in many cultures, talking about death and end-of-life options are taboo, and discussions around these topics are stifled, often close-minded, and polarized. Some people are afraid of dying. Others are afraid of having a painful, horrible death, and still others are being forced to live a torturous life while conditions progressively worsen. The rampant rise of unnecessary cosmetic and plastic surgeries intensifies the angst surrounding death as people attempt to stave off and disguise the normal aging process.

Americans, who lag behind other countries in right to die options, have to live against their wishes, even when they've witnessed tormenting deaths or are in protracted agony themselves.

"The American Medical Association (AMA) is supposedly against physician-assisted suicide because a doctor's pledge is supposed to be to do no harm. However, medical lobbyists and medical boards protect bad doctors, not consumers. This has resulted in medical negligence being a leading cause of death and bodily harm. Negligent doctors are rarely disciplined, and scams and unnecessary procedures continue because of their extraordinary profitability.

"Instead of opposing a compassionate right to die, the AMA should step up to stop preventable iatrogenic harm, which often causes severe and progressive conditions that are without remediation. This is what happened to my husband Tucker. Harmed by a crack-addicted doctor who didn't tell us the truth about what he was going to do, he ended my husband's quality of life.

"Forcing people to exist in hellish situations is doing harm. About a fifth of elderly Americans undergo surgical procedures in hospitals in the last month of their lives. This financially feeds the medical industry. For those who believe in an individual's right to choose what happens to their body, opening up the conversation to include the death option is necessary."

I heard rustling in the crowd. I knew some people would be angered by what I have to say. I thought about Neil and how my support for the right to die upset him. I didn't want to be a spokesperson for this, but this issue chose me through Madeleine, Henry, and Tucker.

"A segment of the population says all life is sacred and needs to be preserved if possible - no matter what – but what about the people who are on death row or victims of war? We teach soldiers to kill, but we refuse someone enduring unbearable agony the right to die peacefully?

"We are expected to end the lives of our pets as an act of mercy. I put down our dog Socrates last week. He was sick and in pain. Everyone supported me doing this. People talk about a Rainbow Bridge as though their pets are finally frolicking in freedom. Meanwhile, in Ireland, the most common method elderly people use to die by their own hand is hanging - a horrible death. By 2016, euthanasia accounted for four percent of total deaths in the Netherlands, where it is legal."

Someone I didn't know left the store. I froze until I saw encouraging nods from the crowd.

"In 1990, the U.S. Supreme Court decided that any competent individual had the right to refuse medical treatment, regardless of prognosis or how effective a treatment might be, but they do not allow choice in how and when we die." A wave of grief washed over me as I looked around my store – Lena's store. I forgot what I had been saying. Jack, who was in a new relationship with Rosemary, jumped up to steady me. I shook my head. *I have to do this on my own.*

"Some doctors have become proponents for the right to die. Doctors, religious leaders, and politicians debate issues of allowing physicians to help terminally ill patients kill themselves. Why does society give these few sectors authority to force people to endure agony because of their dogmas and fears? *Rights and wishes of the ill and others who suffer need to be respected.*"

The crowd applauded.

"Hastening one's death is legal, however, but the freedom to talk about it is *stigmatized* and met with *misjudgments, forced medical treatment, or toxic positivity* instead of *empathy and acceptance.* Also, non-violent means to end life have been outlawed so people with rational reasons may resort to violent means and secrecy, which traumatize and haunt survivors.

"My best friend Madeleine left this world in a brutal manner because she had no other way out after years of debilitating illness.

She was going to run this bookshop with me. She was my biggest cheerleader and came up with the name Bean There. Madeleine loved life, pets, and people, but sadly, she got sick, and when there was no healing to be had, she hung herself."

Murmurs rippled through the rows of people. Lena, Ty, Rosie, Jack, and Jared nodded their approval to me. Ty blew his nose into a white handkerchief he used to make into rabbit shadows on the wall for Madeleine and me when we were three. Geneviève, Mandrel, and Robby sat together, shoulders back, looking proud. A couple in their late seventies headed out the door. The woman made tusking sounds on her way out. The man looked apologetic. He was frail and walked with a cane. I wondered what kind of death he might eventually face.

Two women in their twenties got up and occupied the seats the elder couple had vacated. They leaned forward, ready to hear more. Buoyed by the spirits of Tucker, Madeleine, and Henry, I continued.

"In 1994, Oregon residents passed Measure 16, making the state the first place in the world to legalize, by vote, medical aid in dying or physician-assisted death. But Oregon-style death-with-dignity laws apply only to people who are deemed terminal within six months. This would not have been granted to Madeleine, my grandfather, or Tucker, who was severely damaged by hernia mesh. My loved ones were mentally competent, suffering unbearably with illness or pain, but they wouldn't have met the eligibility criteria IF they lived in a death-with-dignity state."

Chris, a regular patron, lover of Sci Fi, whispered to his partner Lee, "That's terrible."

"Those who support the right to die say state laws are arbitrary and unfair. Some also say death should not be left up to doctors; it's an individual's choice. Right to die opponents are afraid of a slippery slope that will include the sick, mentally ill, elderly, and disabled.

"Some opponents object based on their religion. In various traditions, however, ending one's own life under certain conditions is considered brave or noble. Nobel Peace Prize laureate Desmond Tutu, for example, expressed the desire to have the option of an assisted death. Under the Freedom of Religion Act, an individual *ought to have the right to choose.*"

Lee leaned back into Chris and said, "I want the right to choose."

"In the DSM - the Diagnostic and Statistical Manual of Mental Disorders - suicide (a stigmatized word), is described as a symptom of mental illness. It's rational, however, to desire to be released from unbearable pain. *Mad in America: Bad Science, Bad Medicine, and the Enduring Mistreatment of the Mentally Ill,* by award-winning journalist Robert Whitaker, shines light on the misguided DSM. Bean There is and will remain stocked up on this excellent book.

Many of you knew Tucker. He came to every Living Story Night for years, volunteered, and gave concerts at the community center and was always ready to help someone. At thirty-six, he was shut in the house due to medical harm. Tucker asked his doctor to grant a compassionate death. The doctor said, 'I would, but it's illegal for me to. You have so much to live for.' But did he? How many of you would want to live in untenable pain without a moment of reprieve?

"There were many wonderful things in my life I would love to share with you, but the right to die issue has taken over my life. I watched my dearest loved ones suffer needlessly. Many people are one bad death away from becoming a right to die advocate. To that end, I've researched and gathered together the best books on death with dignity and medical malpractice. Lena and Ty will keep this section going. Thank you for listening. I love all of you."

My last call on my last day at the talk line was a special one.

"Hello, North Yarmouth Grief and Support Call Line. This is Angela. What's your name?"

"Hi, Angela, it's Kieran."

"Kieran! How are you? I think about you and Mary Rose often. "Fly Me to The Moon"?"

"Maybe something different tonight."

"Sure. Do you want to talk?"

"I'm missing my mother. It's a hard night. One of those *I don't know if I can get through this night* nights. I was wondering if..."

"Yes?'

"Do you by any chance know "Too-Ra-Loo-Ra-Loo-Ra"?"

"I sure do, man. Are you going to sing with me?

"When I'm not crying, I'll try. You sing for Tucker, and I'll sing for Ma."

We sang in harmony,

Over in Killarney
Many years ago,
Me Mither sang a song to me
In tones so sweet and low.
Just a simple little ditty,
In her good ould Irish way,
And I'd give the world if she could sing
That song to me this day.
"Too-ra-loo-ra-loo-ral, Too-ra-loo-ra-li,
Too-ra-loo-ra-loo-ral, hush now, don't you cry!
Too-ra-loo-ra-loo-ral, Too-ra-loo-ra-li,
Too-ra-loo-ra-loo-ral, that's an Irish lullaby."
Oft in dreams I wander
To that cot again,
I feel her arms a-huggin' me
As when she held me then.
And I hear her voice a -hummin'
To me as in days of yore,
When she used to rock me fast asleep
Outside the cabin door.

"Thank you."

"You're welcome, Kieran. Thank you, too."

Click.

EPILOGUE

My skin had tanned a tawny brown, the color of a darkened sky during sunset. Red petals danced overhead. The fog was so thick I could write my name ANGELA ALEXANDER BOYD with my finger, and in my mind, it lingered, then evaporated like fairy dust onto the grass below.

Hoofing through two continents in three months, I hadn't found what I was looking for: a reason my husband had to die so young. An icy tempestuous gust kicked up and licked my face.

I reflected on the chapters of my life: Madeleine and the dollhouse bookshop. Rosemary. Word fasting in my quest to hear. Mourning Madeleine. Earning my degree in psychology. Blossoming into a world traveler, runner, and bookstore owner. Hosting the Living Stories series. Jack, and then not Jack. Meeting that magical blues singer, the mayor of New York, who proposed to me under a crest of Andean Condors on Machu Picchu. Volunteering at the talk line. Helping to found the North Yarmouth Community Support Center. Loving, caring for, and losing Tucker.

There may be many new chapters ahead, or my living story may end unannounced. I no longer know what I want or where I belong. There is nothing to do but follow my breath. I stopped walking. A hawk appeared and spread its wings. *Perhaps*, the wind whispered. I began to dance.

ABOUT THE AUTHOR

Patient safety educator and visual artist Sasha Lauren is author of *The Paris Predicament*, a dramatic, whimsical, feel-good novel about a portrait artist who goes on a journey for meaning and redemption. Sasha is a former massage therapist, Hollywood script consultant, Shakespearean actress, professional organizer, and world traveler. Her second novel, *Final Lullaby*, a love story, is a courageous exploration of the right to die with dignity.

OTHER TITLES BY SASHA LAUREN

WRITERS ASSEMBLED CONTEST WINNER

THE PARIS PREDICAMENT

SASHA LAUREN

NOTE FROM SASHA LAUREN

Word-of-mouth is crucial for any author to succeed. If you enjoyed *Final Lullaby*, please leave a review online—anywhere you are able. Even if it's just a sentence or two. It would make all the difference and would be very much appreciated.

Thanks!
Sasha Lauren

We hope you enjoyed reading this title from:

BLACK ROSE
writing™

Subscribe to our mailing list – *The Rosevine* – and receive **FREE** books, daily deals, and stay current with news about upcoming releases and our hottest authors.
Scan the QR code below to sign up.

Already a subscriber? Please accept a sincere thank you for being a fan of Black Rose Writing authors.

View other Black Rose Writing titles at
www.blackrosewriting.com/books and use promo code
PRINT to receive a **20% discount** when purchasing.